HELLO, HEDGEHOG!

Happy Birthday, Hedgehog!

ACORN™
SCHOLASTIC INC.

Norm Feuti

To Katie, Maria, and Brian — NF

Library of Congress Cataloging-in-Publication Data

Names: Feuti, Norman, author, illustrator.
Title: Happy birthday, Hedgehog! / Norm Feuti.
Description: First edition. | New York : Acorn/Scholastic Inc., 2022. |
Series: Hello, Hedgehog! ; 6 | Audience: Ages 4–6. | Audience: Grades K–1. |
Summary: Harry is worried when he discovers someone has given his best friend, Hedgehog, the exact same birthday gift he brought, but Hedgehog reassures his best pal that since he now has two airplanes, he can race them with Harry.
Identifiers: LCCN 2021033712 (print) |
ISBN 9781338677188 (library binding) | ISBN 9781338677171 (paperback) |
Subjects: CYAC: Birthdays—Fiction. | Parties—Fiction. |
Hedgehogs—Fiction. | Best friends—Fiction. | Friendship—Fiction.
Classification: LCC PZ7.1.F52 Hap 2022 (print) |
DDC [E]—dc23

LC record available at https://lccn.loc.gov/2021033712

10 9 8 7 6 5 4 3 2 1   22 23 24 25 26

Printed in China   62
First edition, May 2022
Edited by Katie Carella
Book design by Maria Mercado

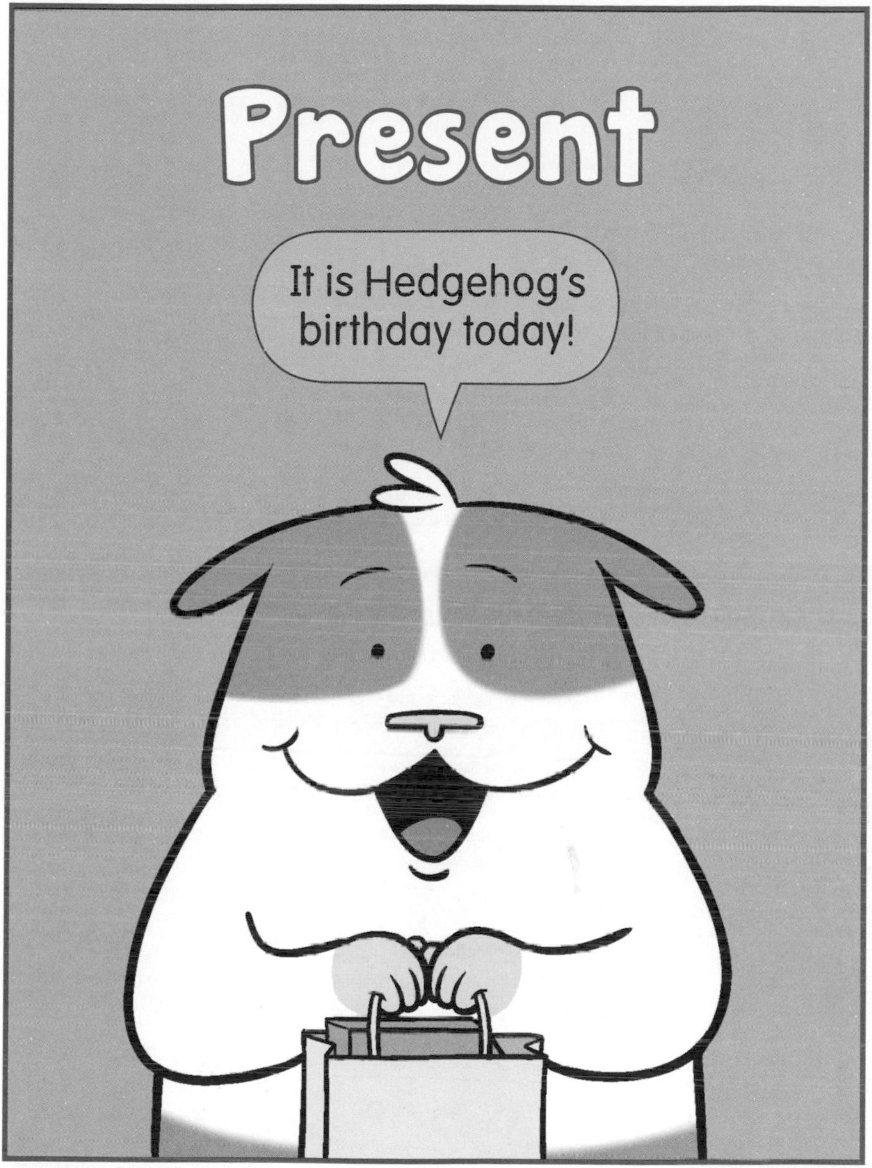
Present
It is Hedgehog's birthday today!

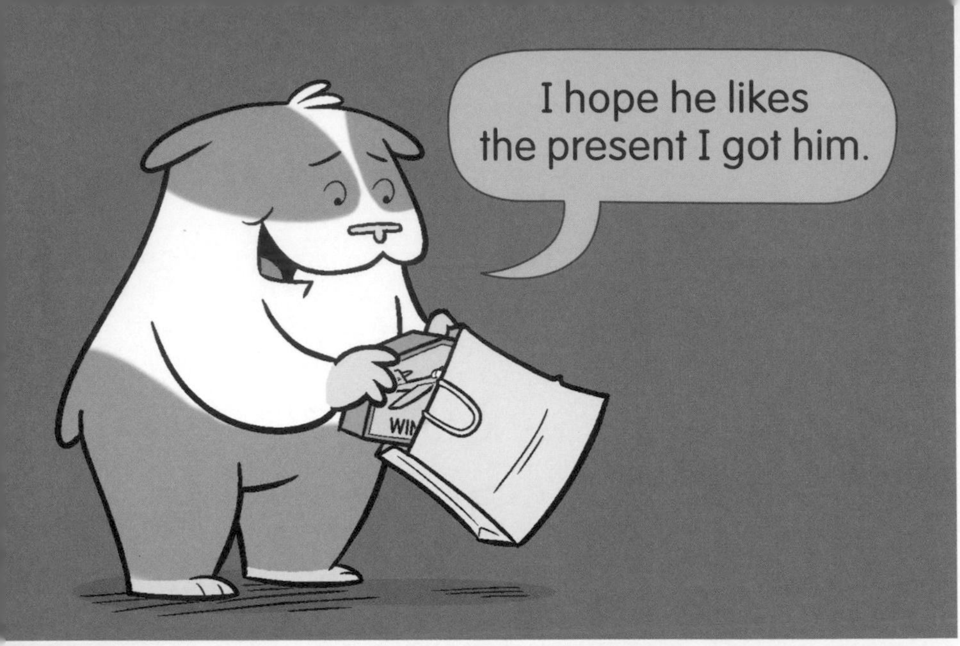
I hope he likes the present I got him.
WIN

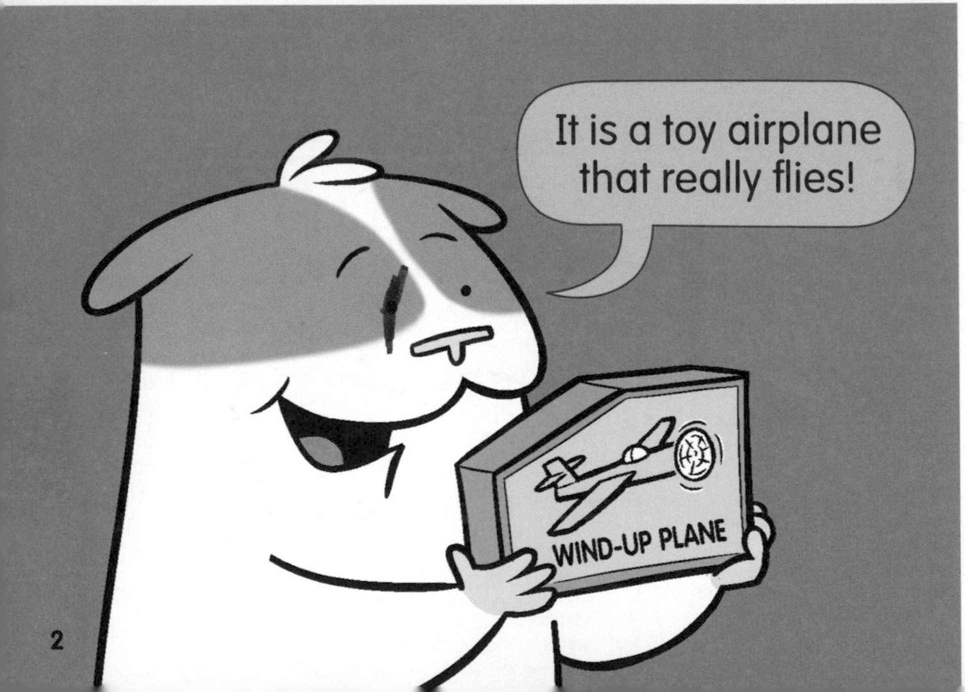
It is a toy airplane that really flies!
WIND-UP PLANE

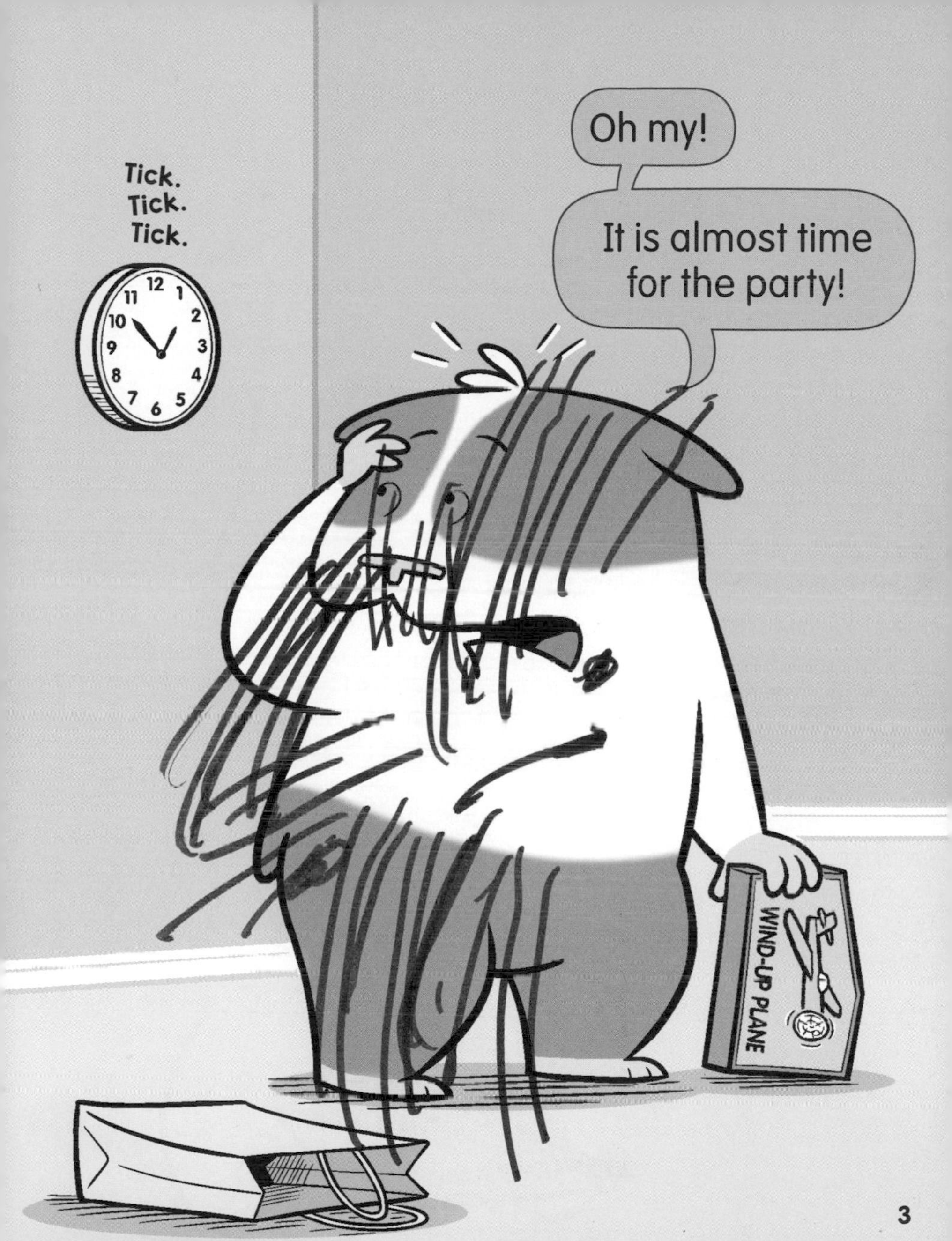
Tick.
Tick.
Tick.
Oh my!
It is almost time for the party!
WIND-UP PLANE

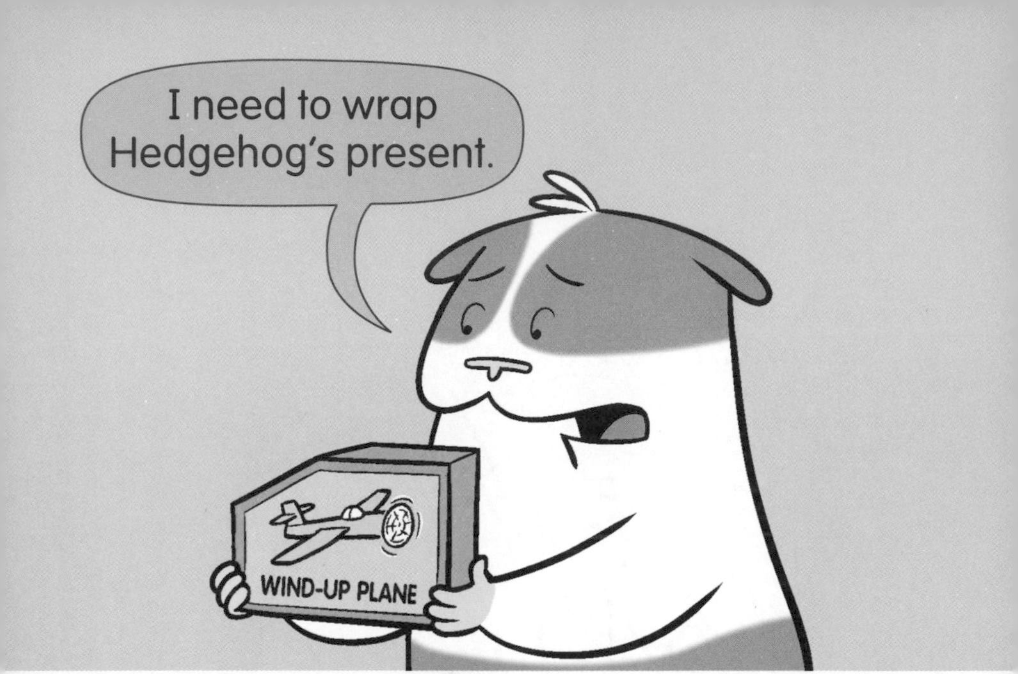
I need to wrap Hedgehog's present.
WIND-UP PLANE

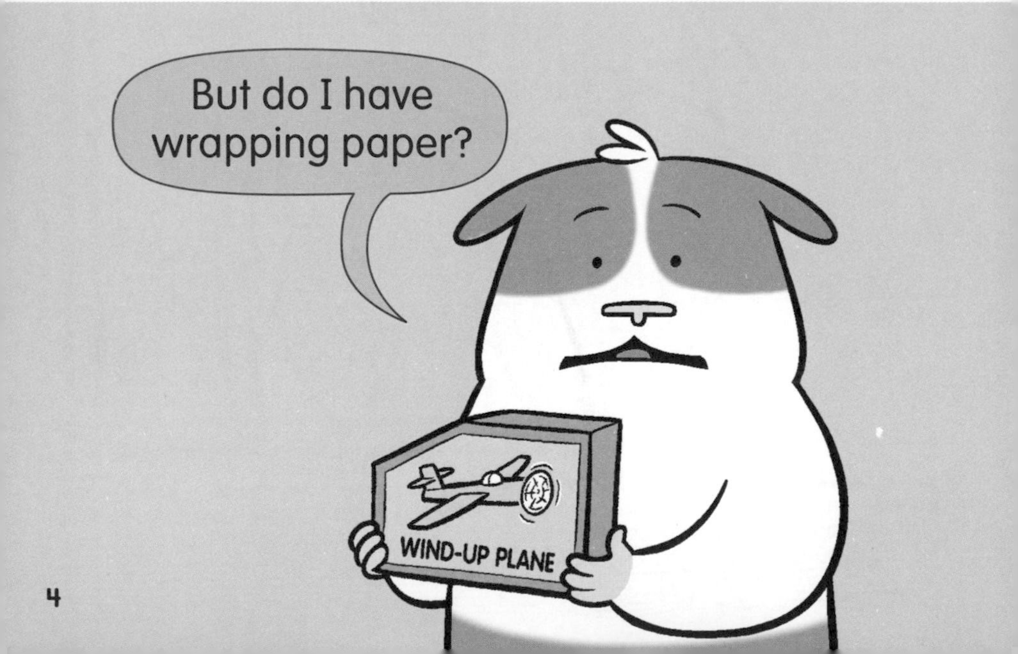
But do I have wrapping paper?
WIND-UP PLANE

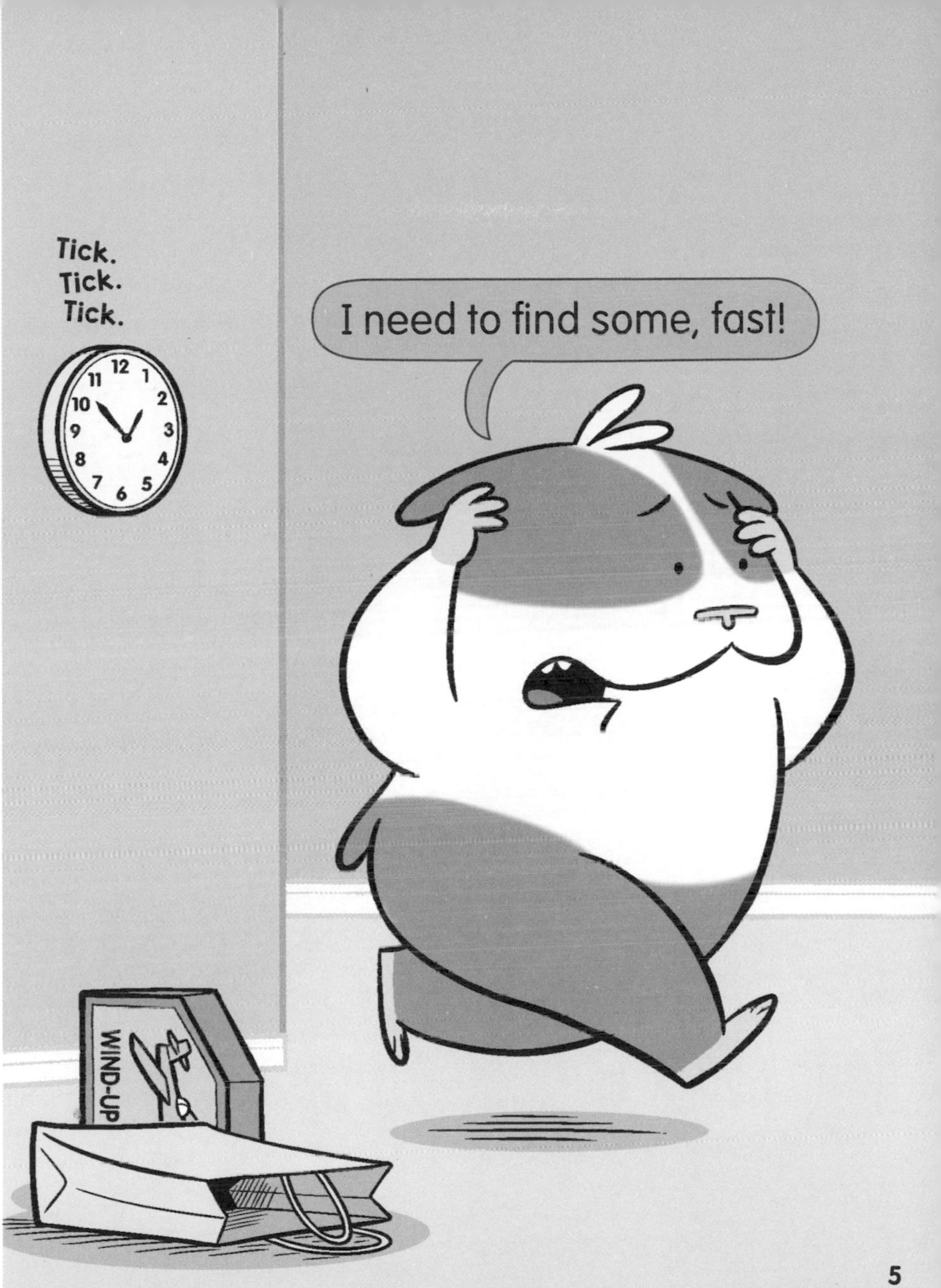
Tick.
Tick.
Tick.
I need to find some, fast!
WIND-UP

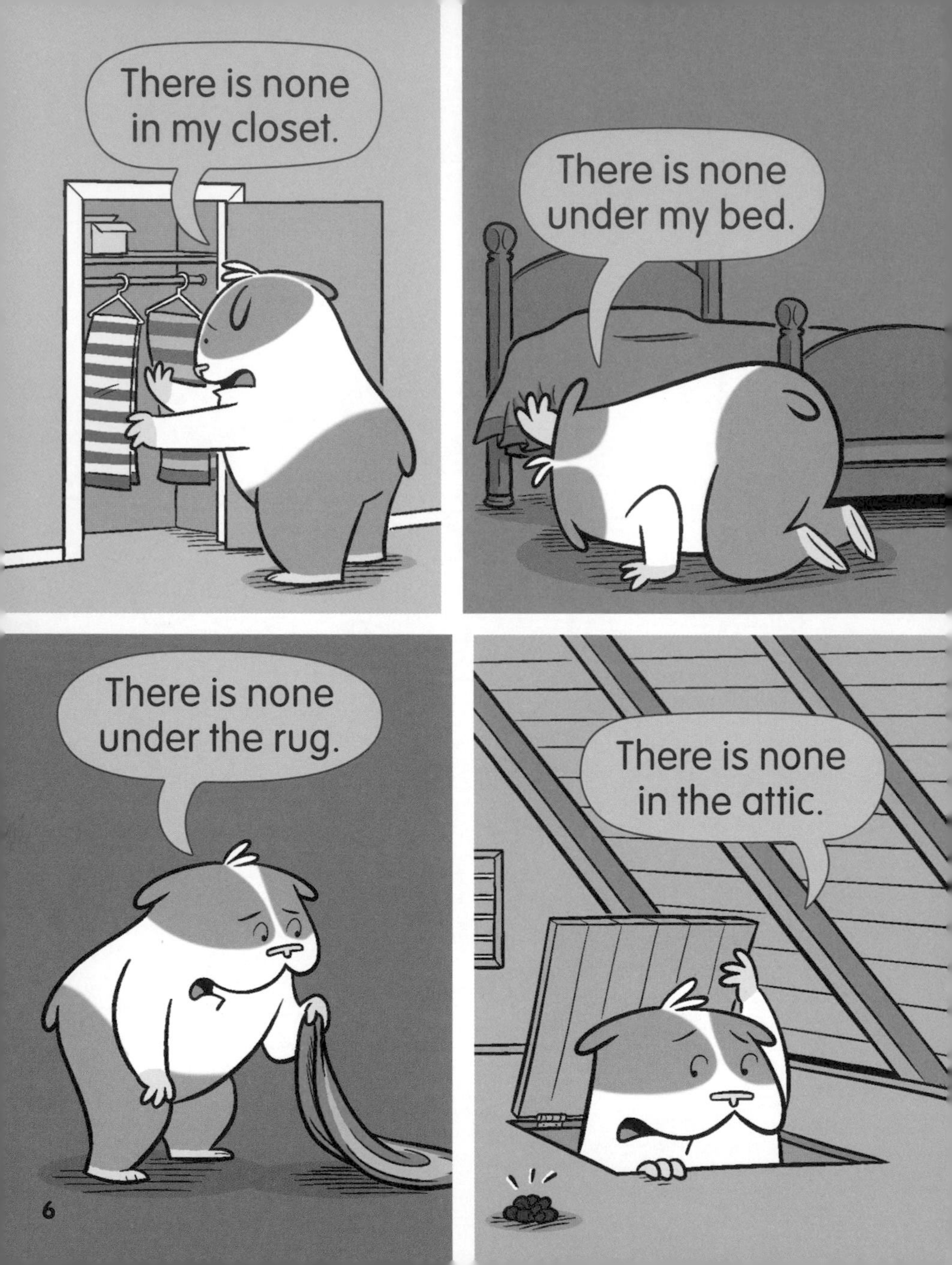
There is none in my closet.
There is none under my bed.
There is none under the rug.
There is none in the attic.

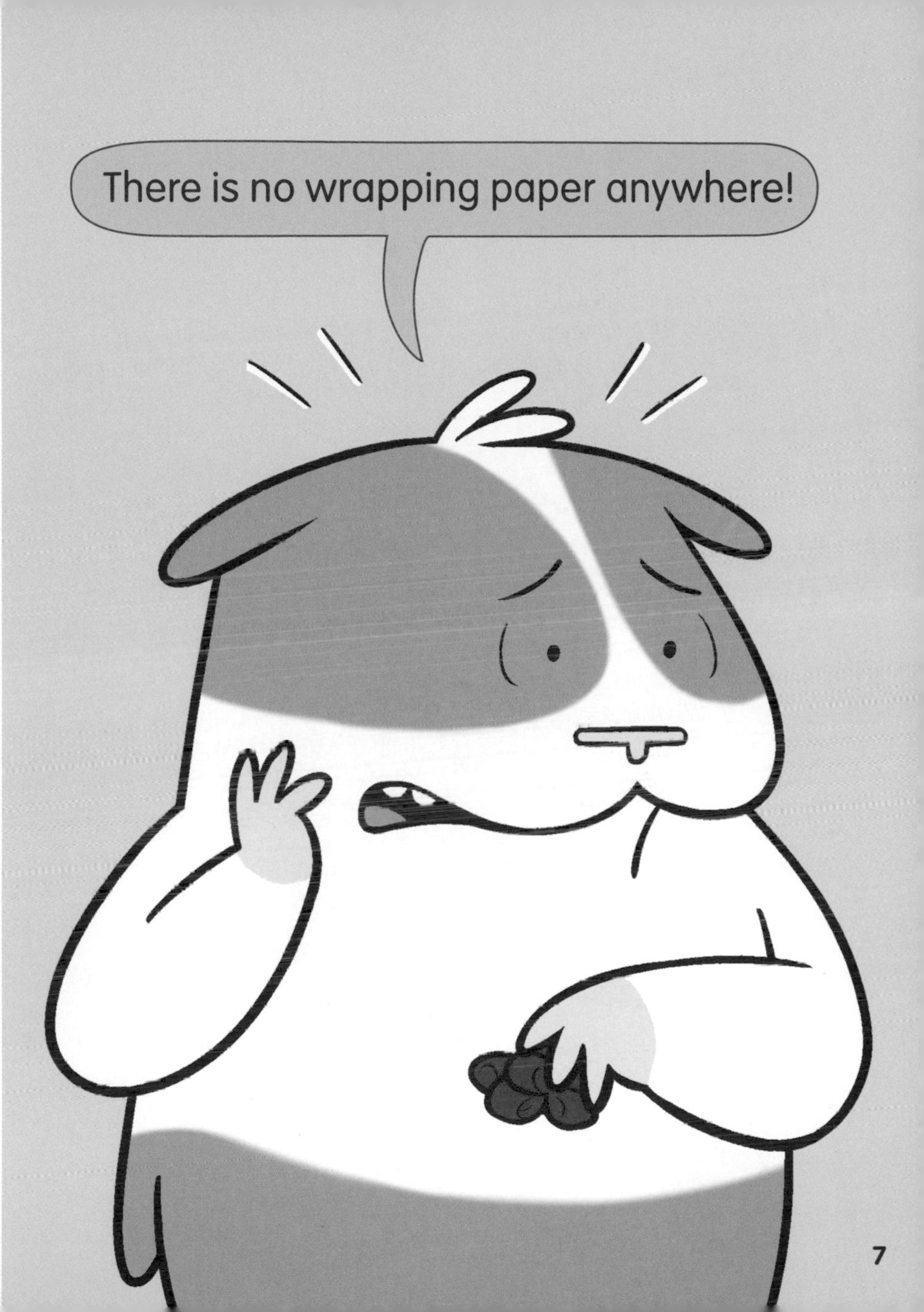
There is no wrapping paper anywhere!

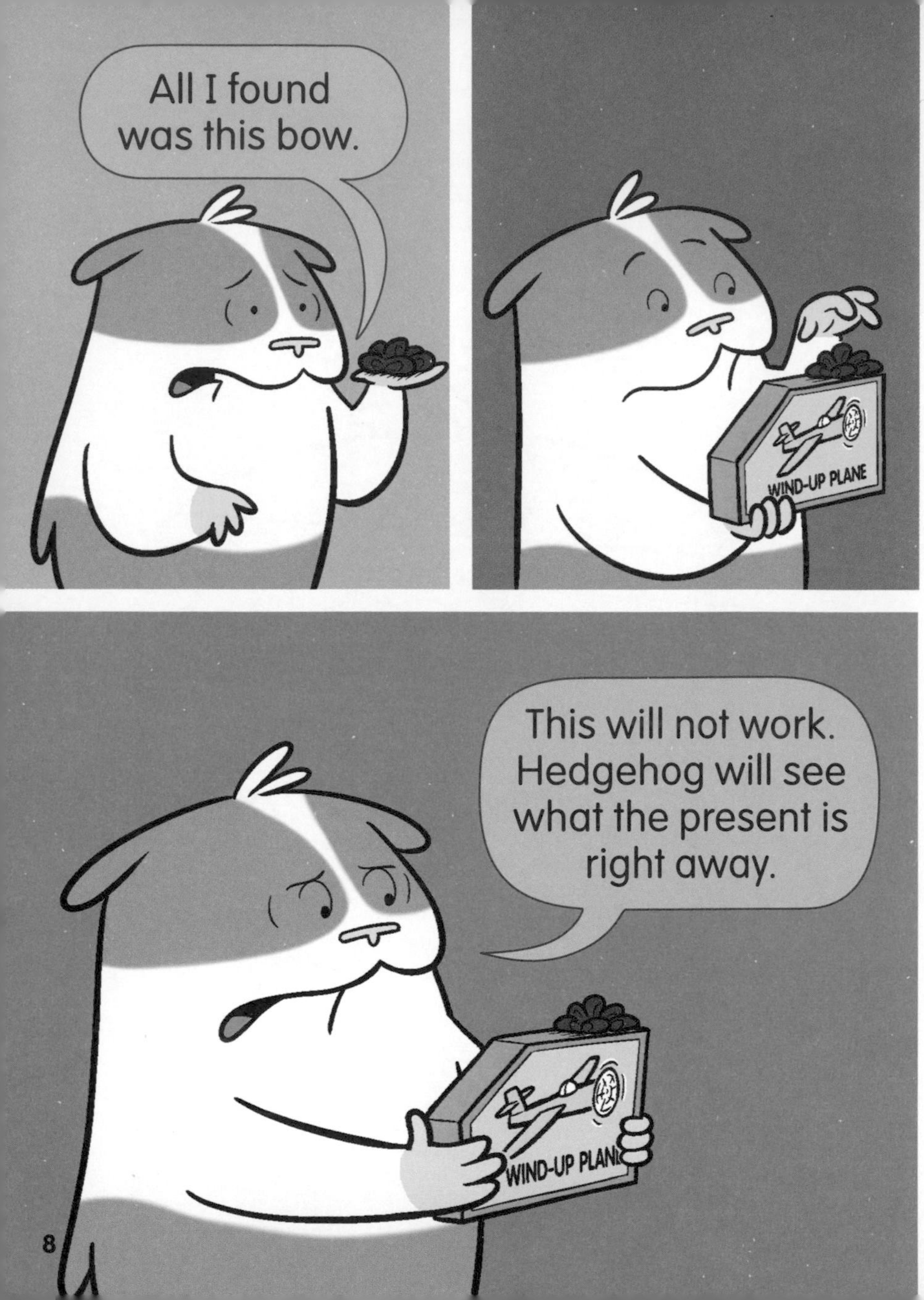
All I found was this bow.
WIND-UP PLANE
This will not work. Hedgehog will see what the present is right away.
WIND-UP PLAN

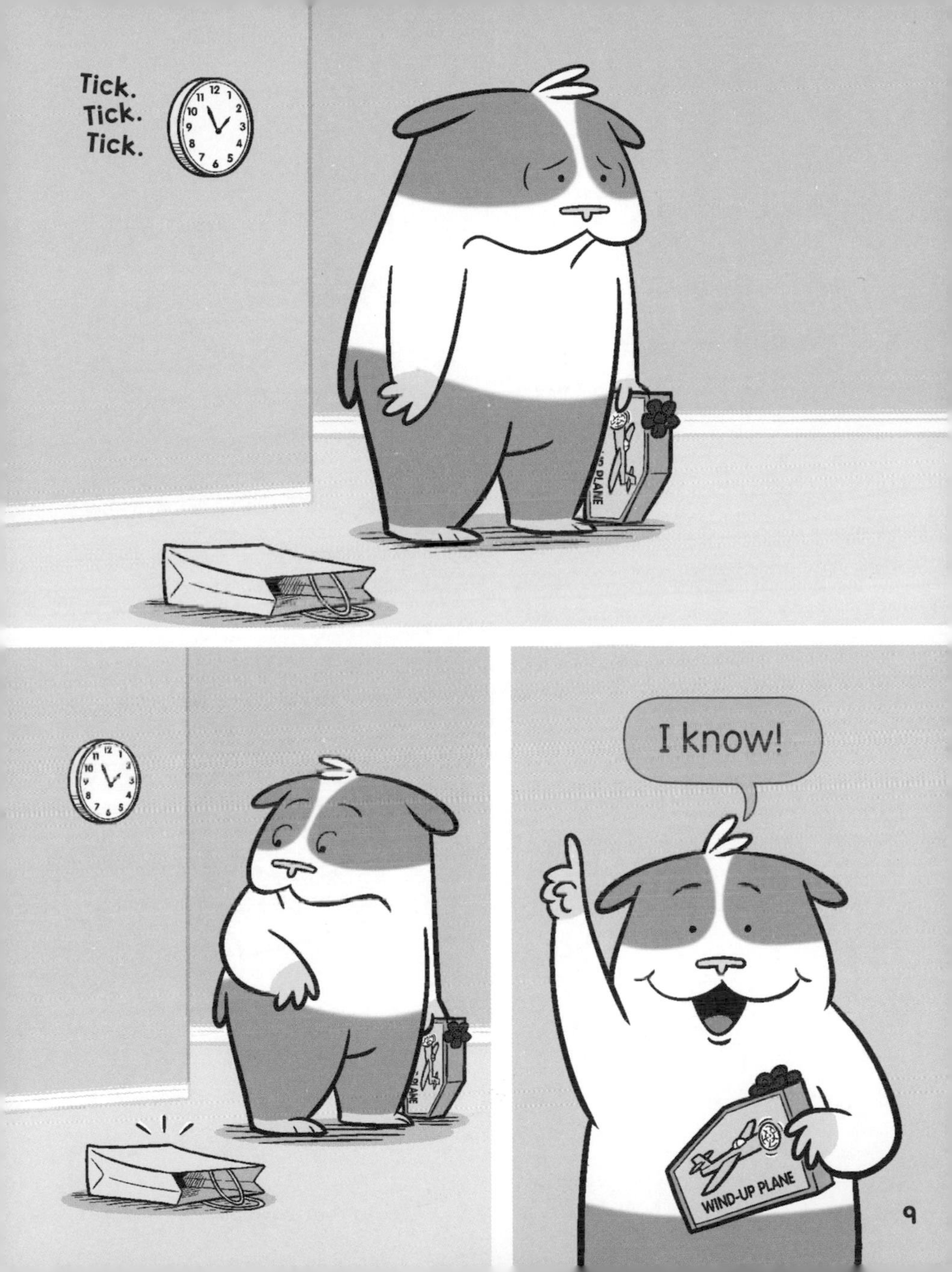
Tick.
Tick.
Tick.
I know!
WIND-UP PLANE

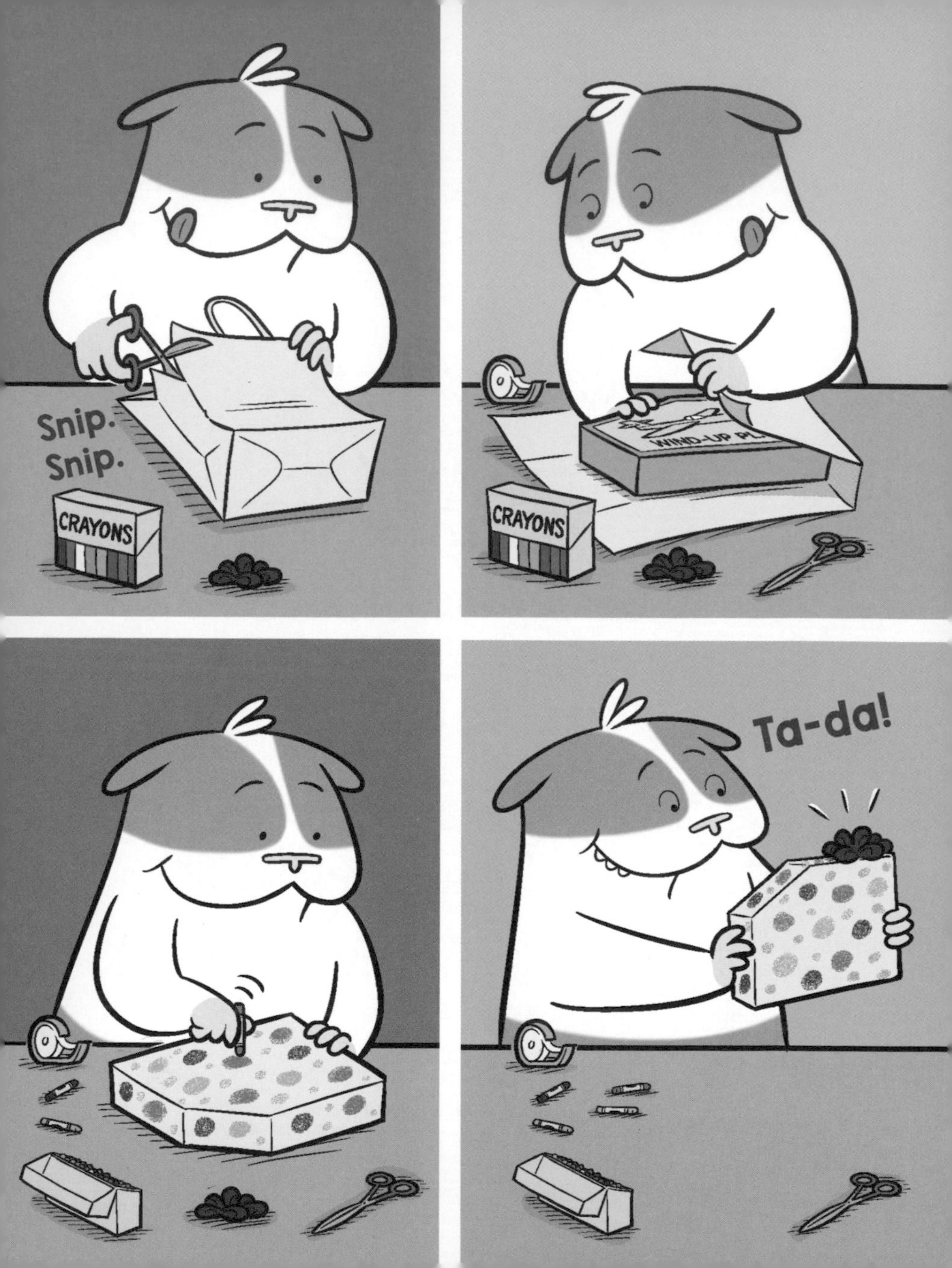
Snip.
Snip.
CRAYONS
CRAYONS
WIND-UP PL
Ta-da!

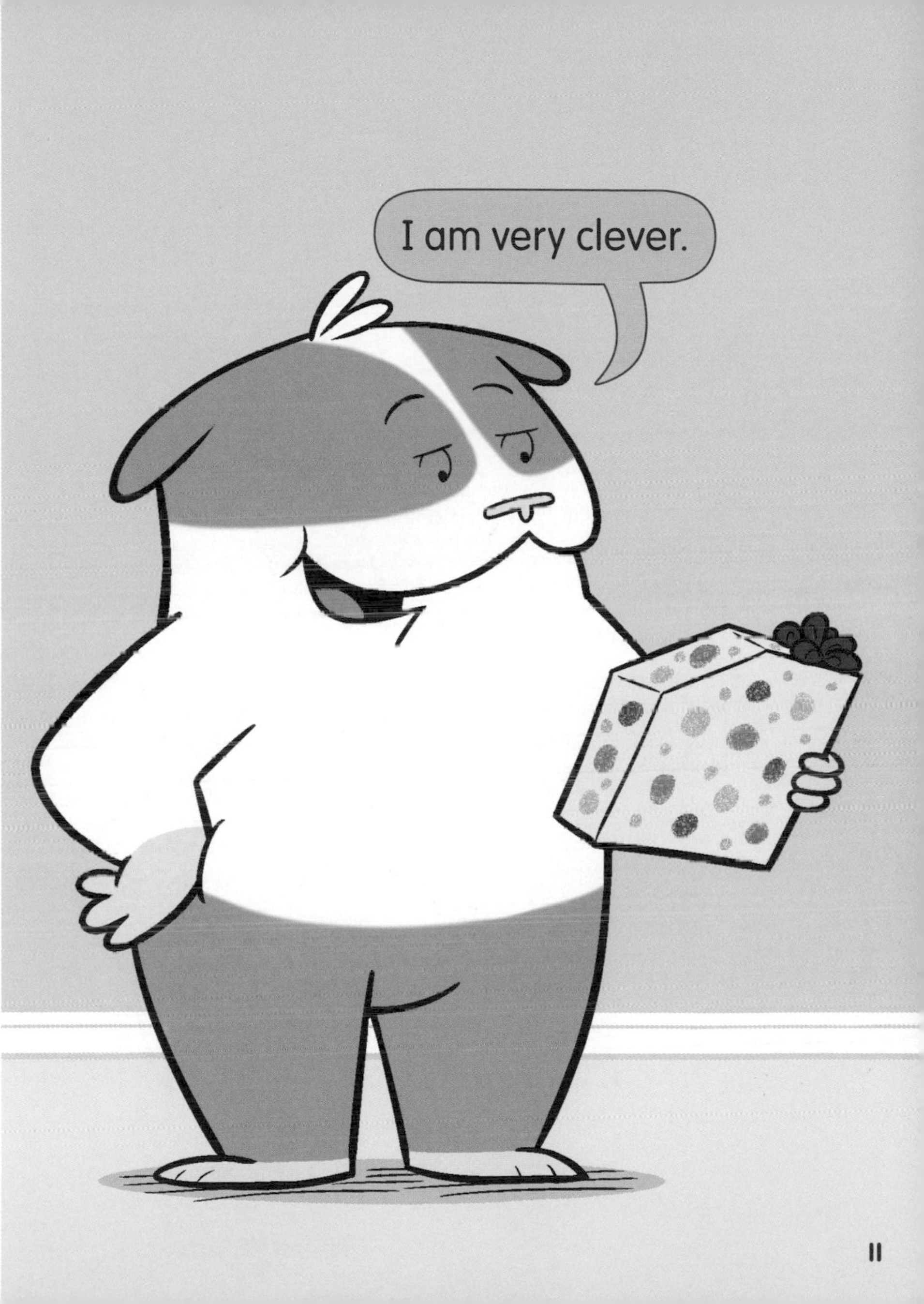
I am very clever.

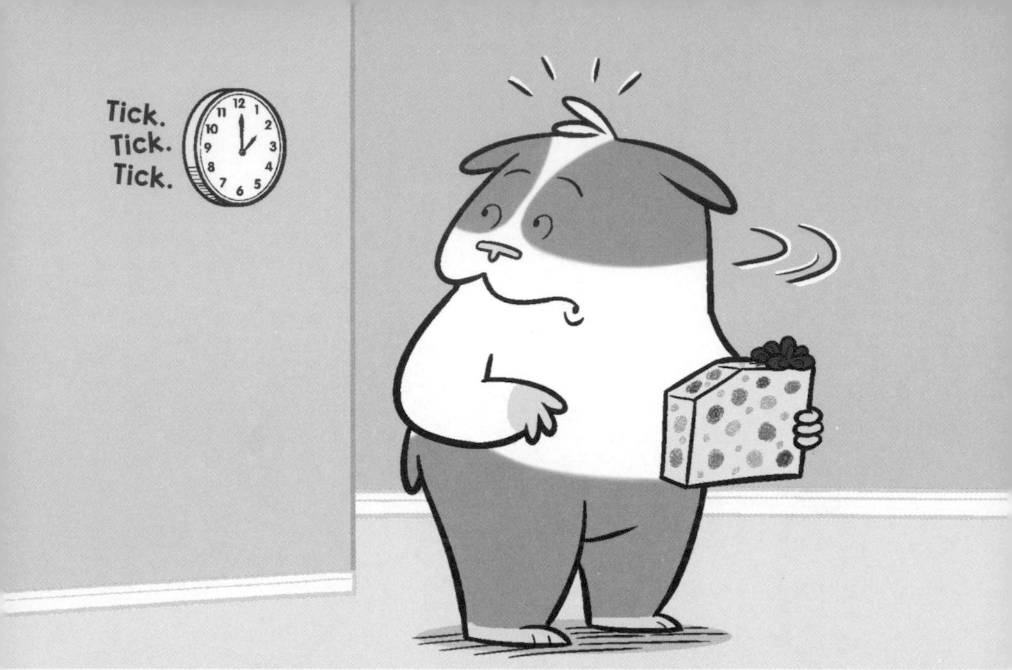
Tick.
Tick.
Tick.

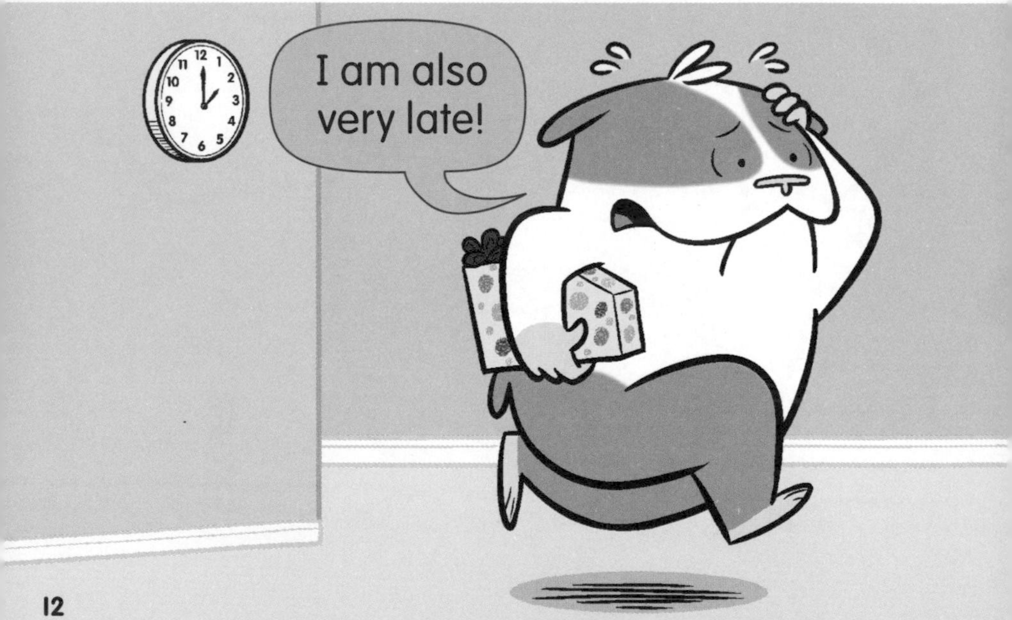
I am also very late!

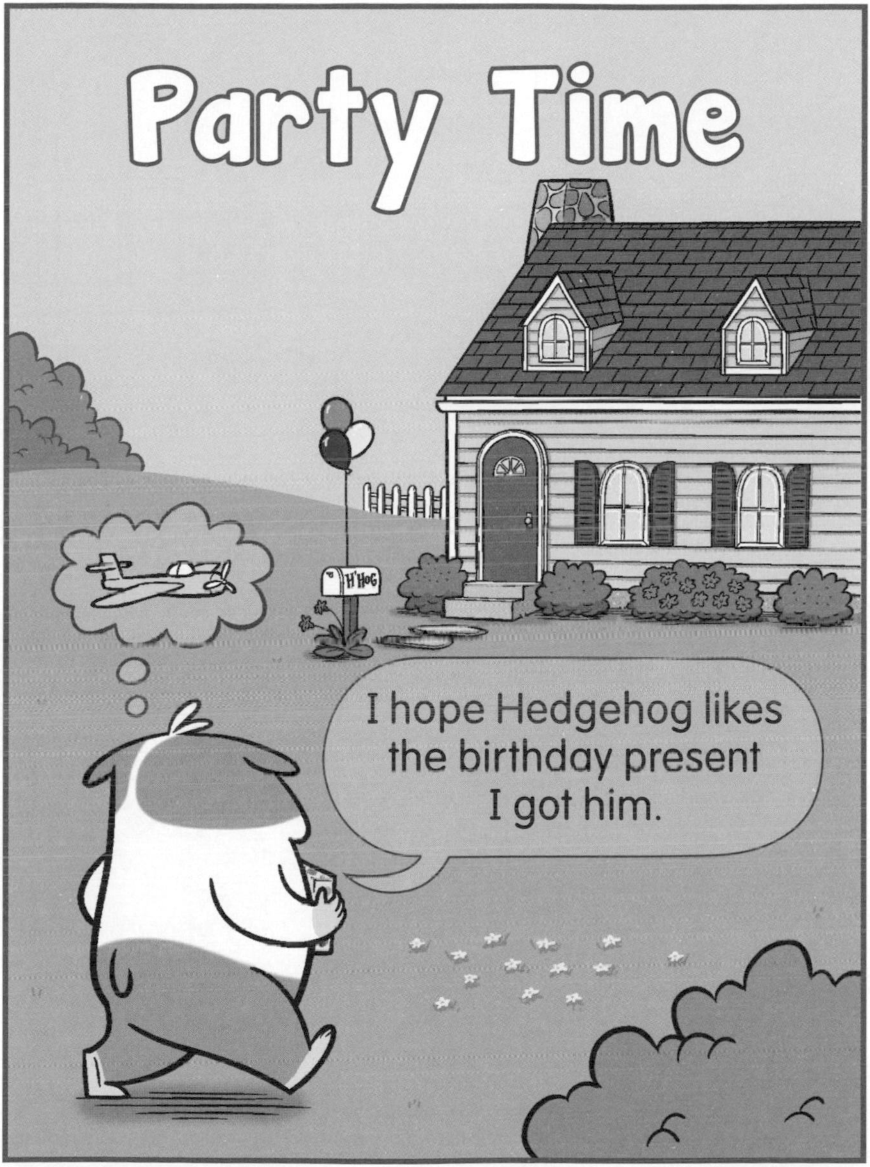
Party Time
H'HOG
I hope Hedgehog likes the birthday present I got him.

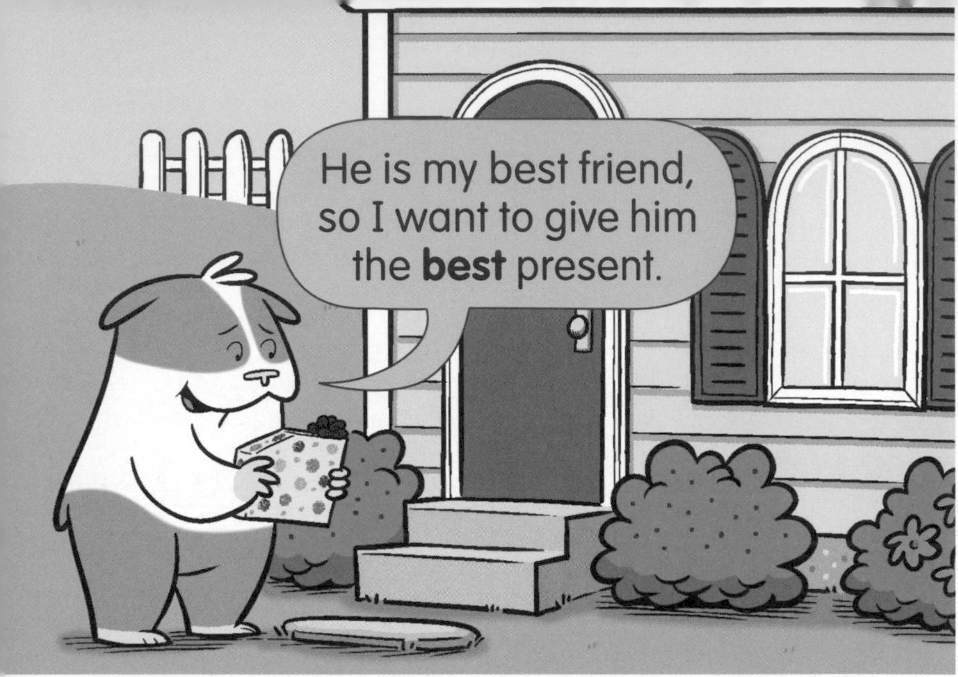
He is my best friend, so I want to give him the **best** present.

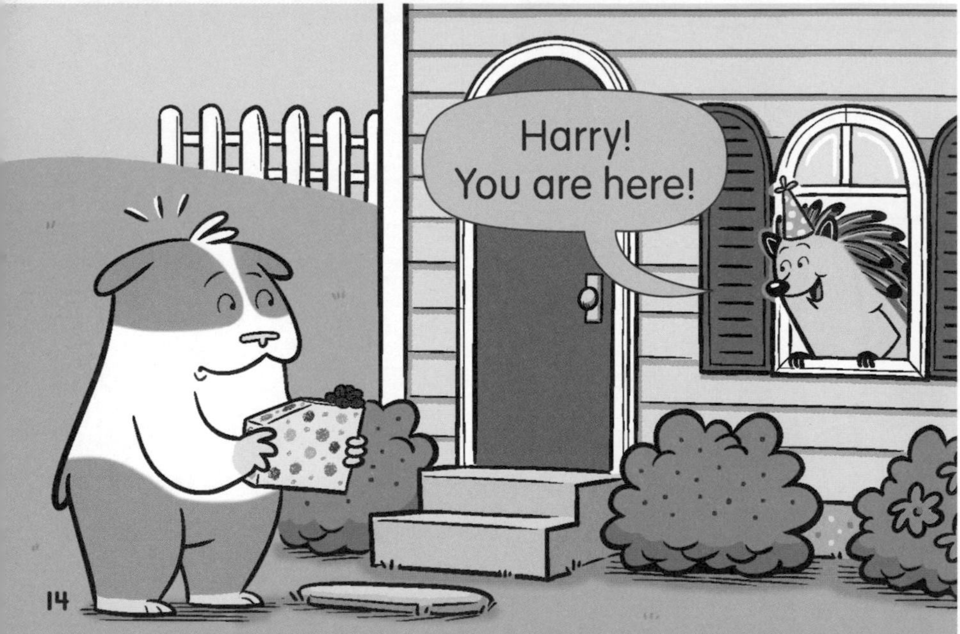
Harry! You are here!

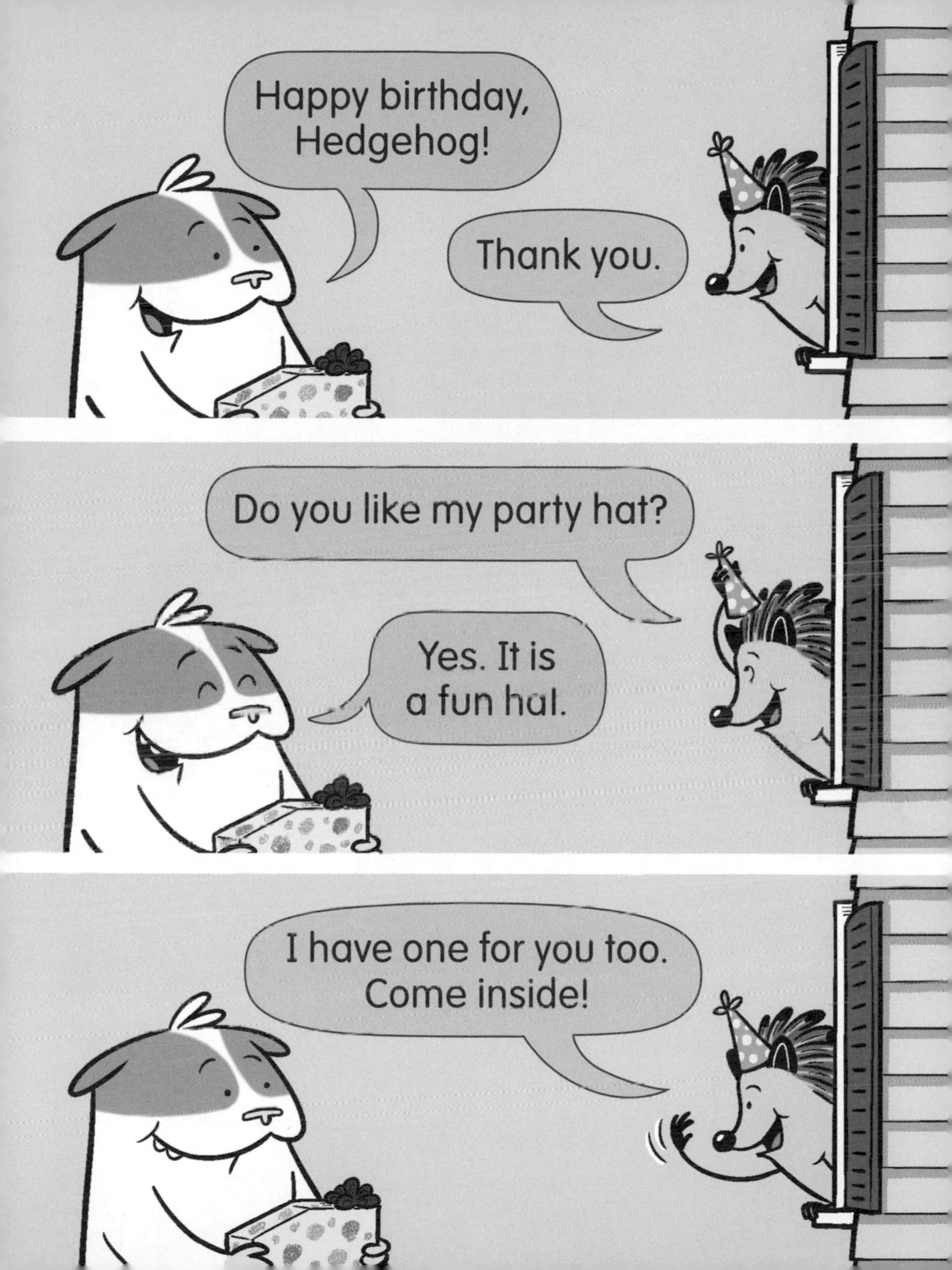
Happy birthday, Hedgehog!
Thank you.
Do you like my party hat?
Yes. It is a fun hat.
I have one for you too. Come inside!

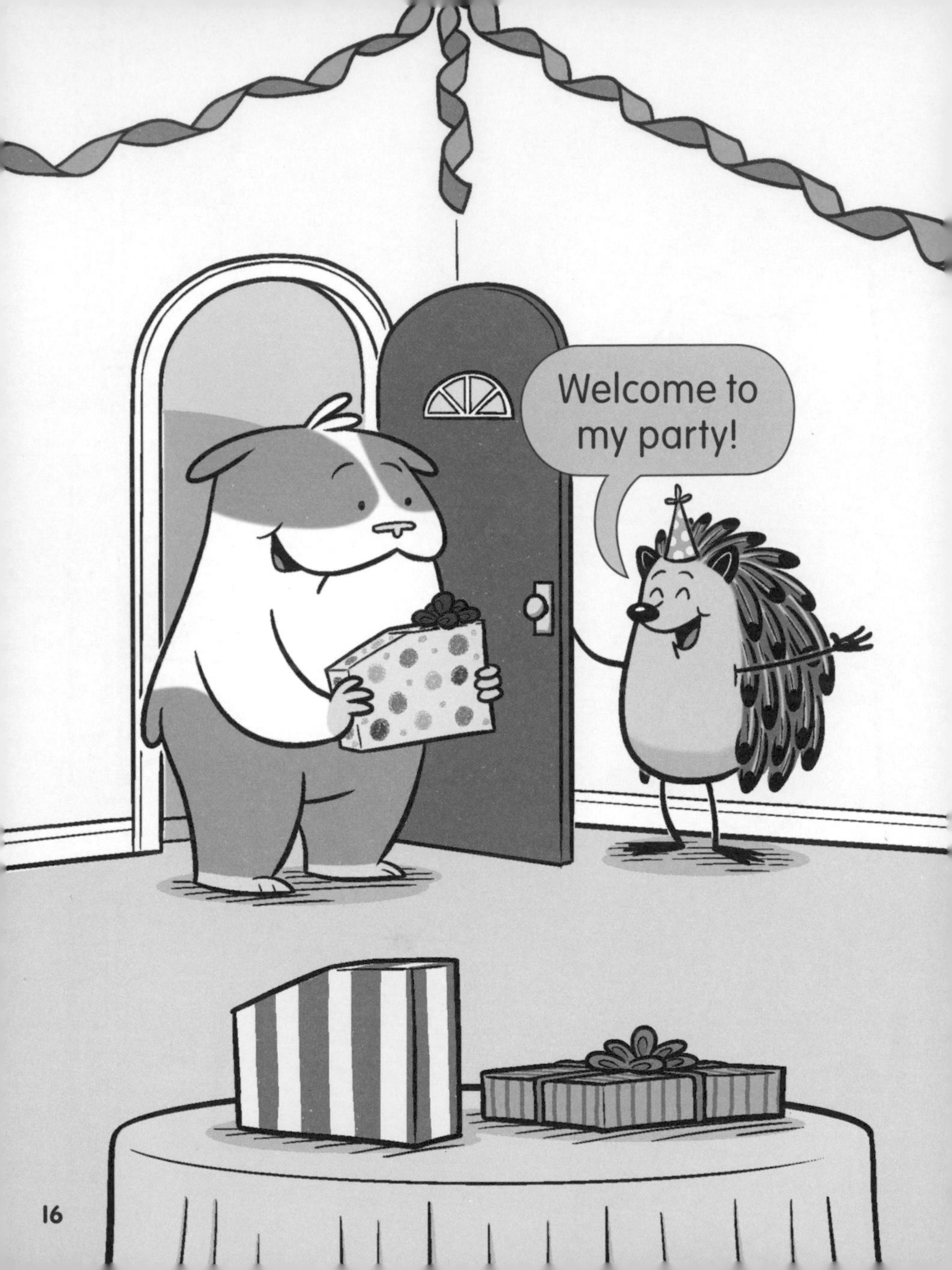
Welcome to my party!

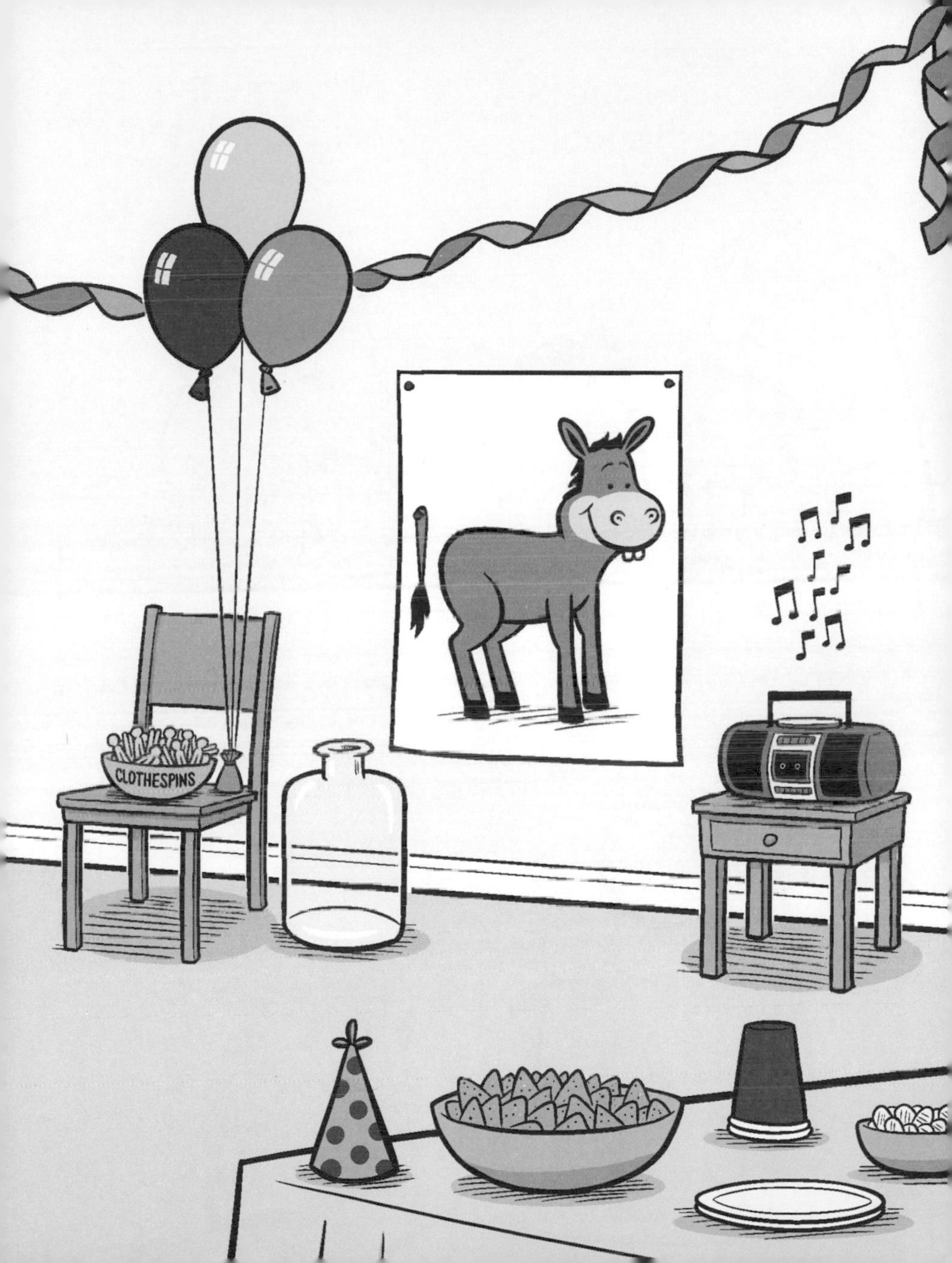
CLOTHESPINS

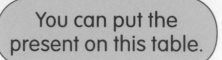
You can put the present on this table.

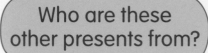
Who are these other presents from?

They are from my friends who live far away.

They came in the mail today!

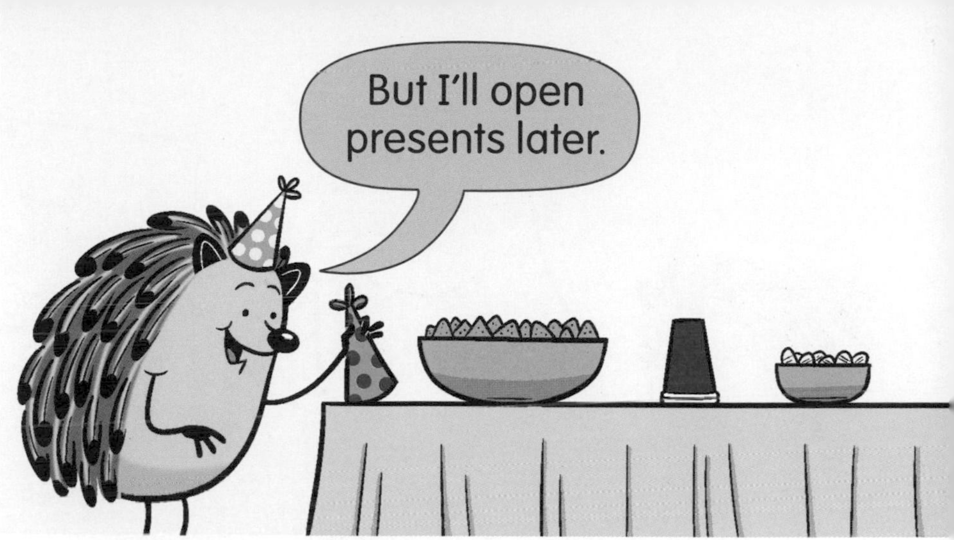

But I'll open presents later.

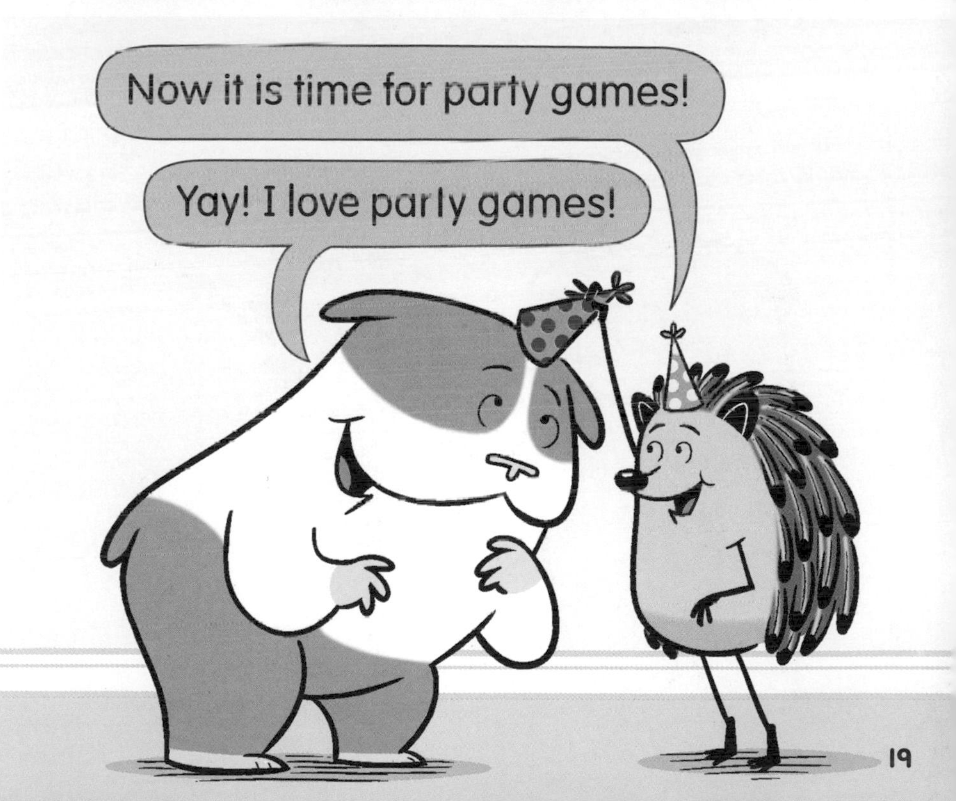

Now it is time for party games!
Yay! I love party games!

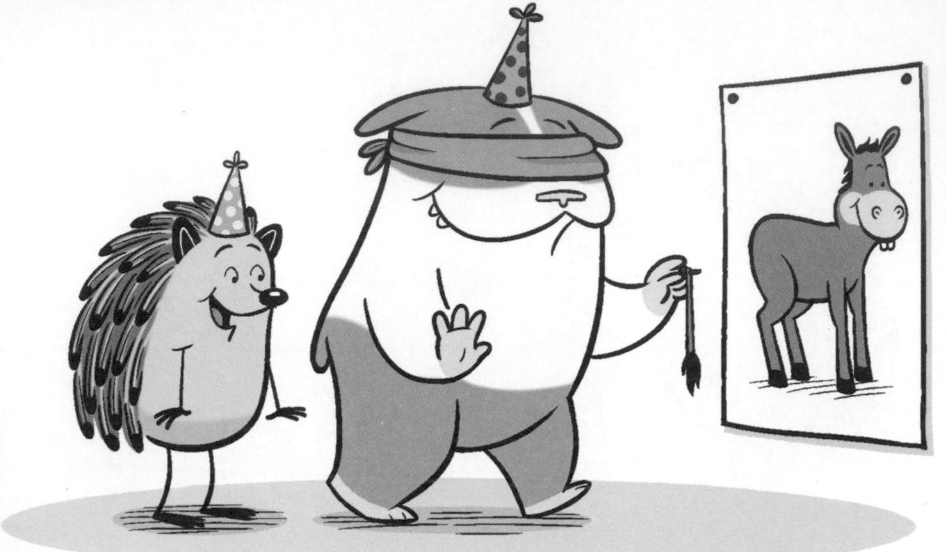

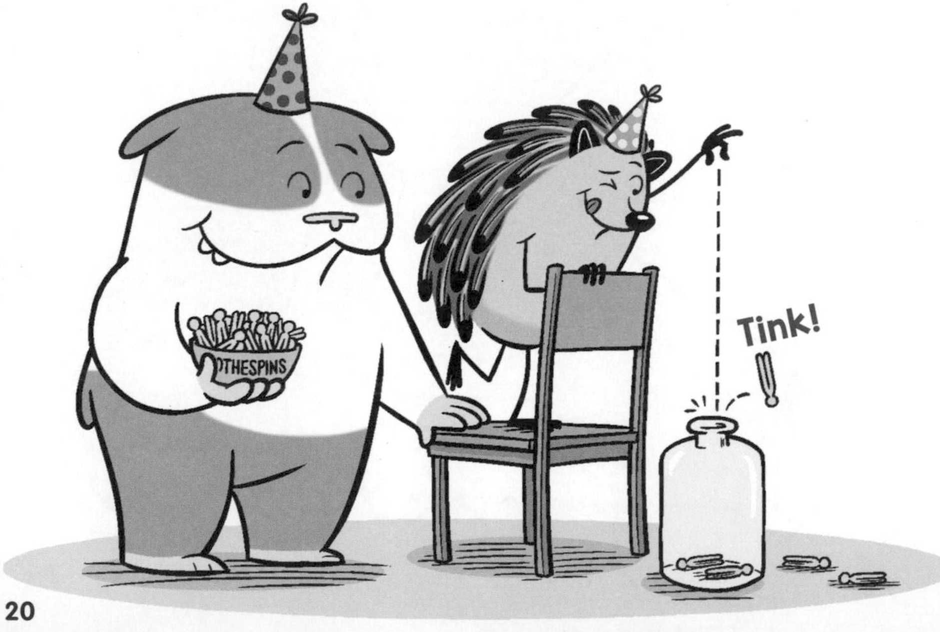

OTHESPINS
Tink!

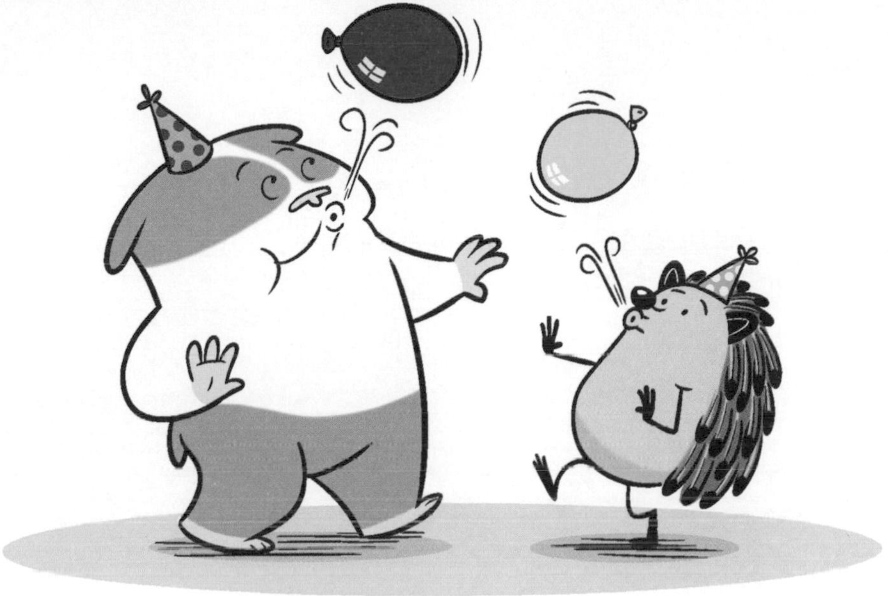

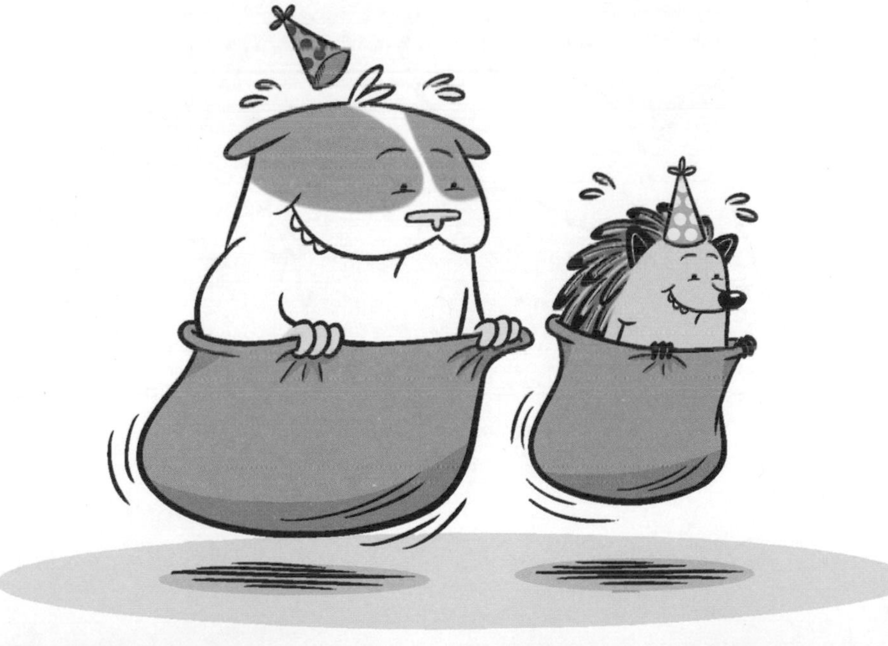

You know how to throw a good party, Hedgehog.
I am glad you are having fun, Harry.

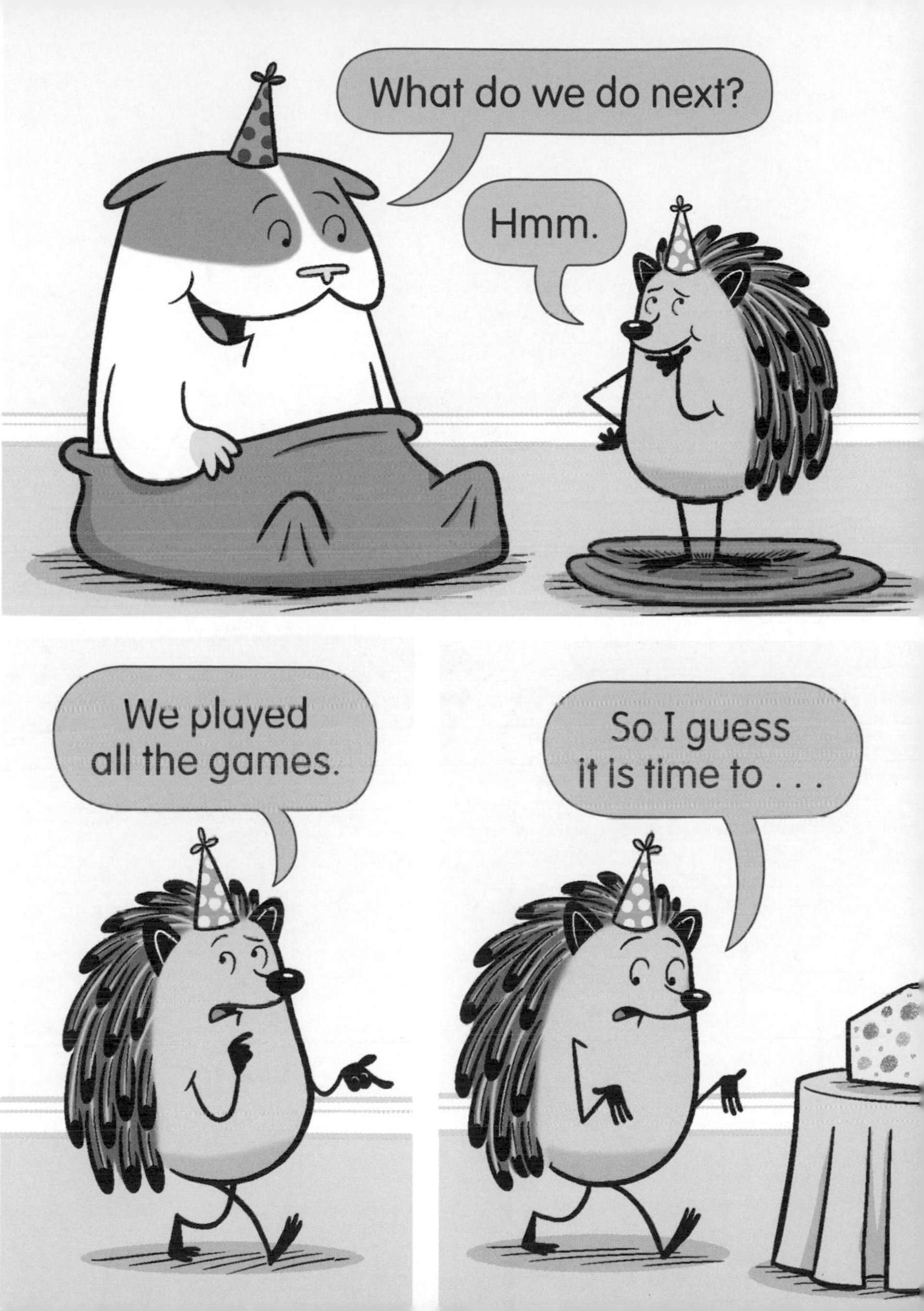
What do we do next?
Hmm.
We played all the games.
So I guess it is time to . . .

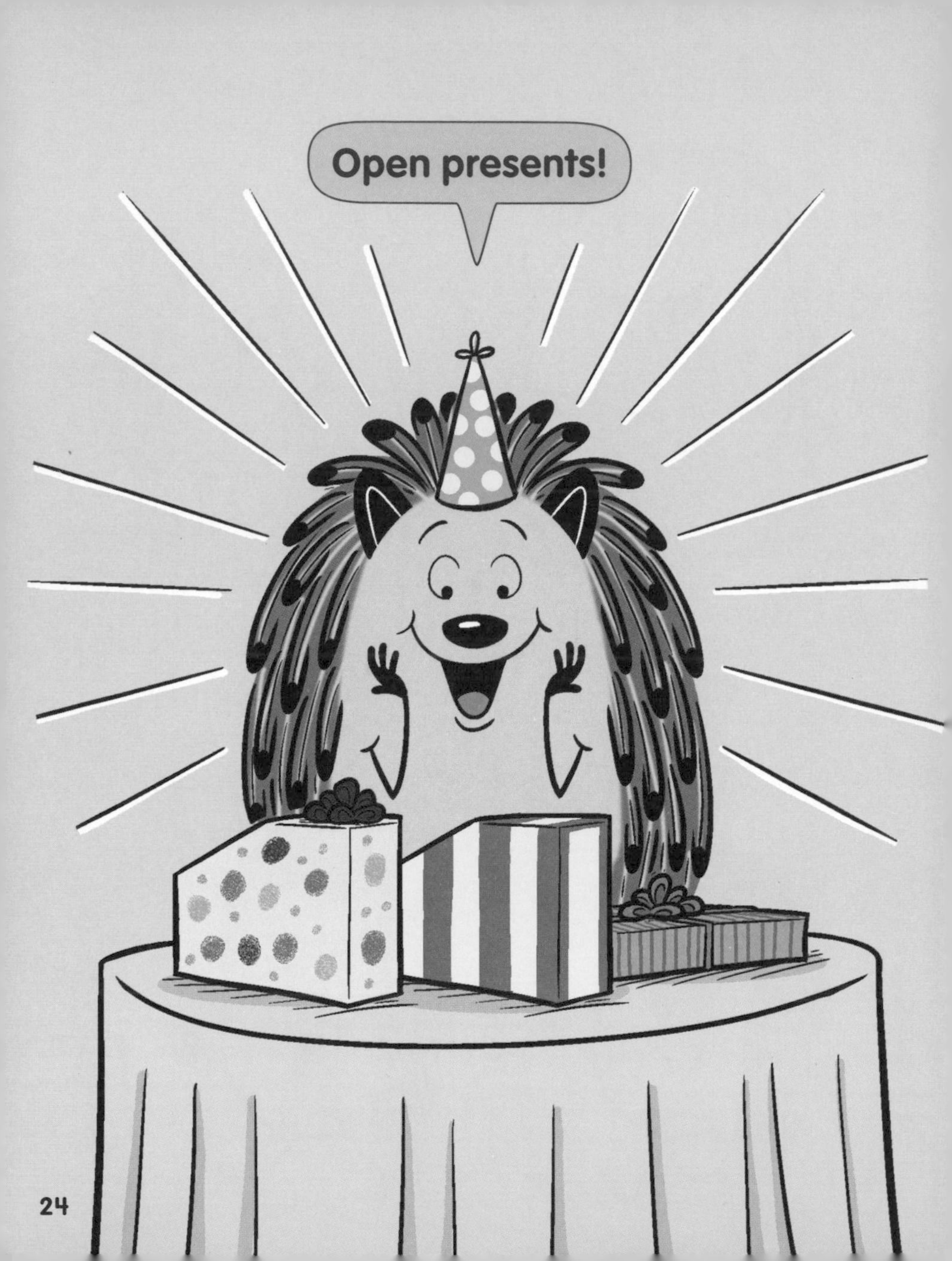
Open presents!

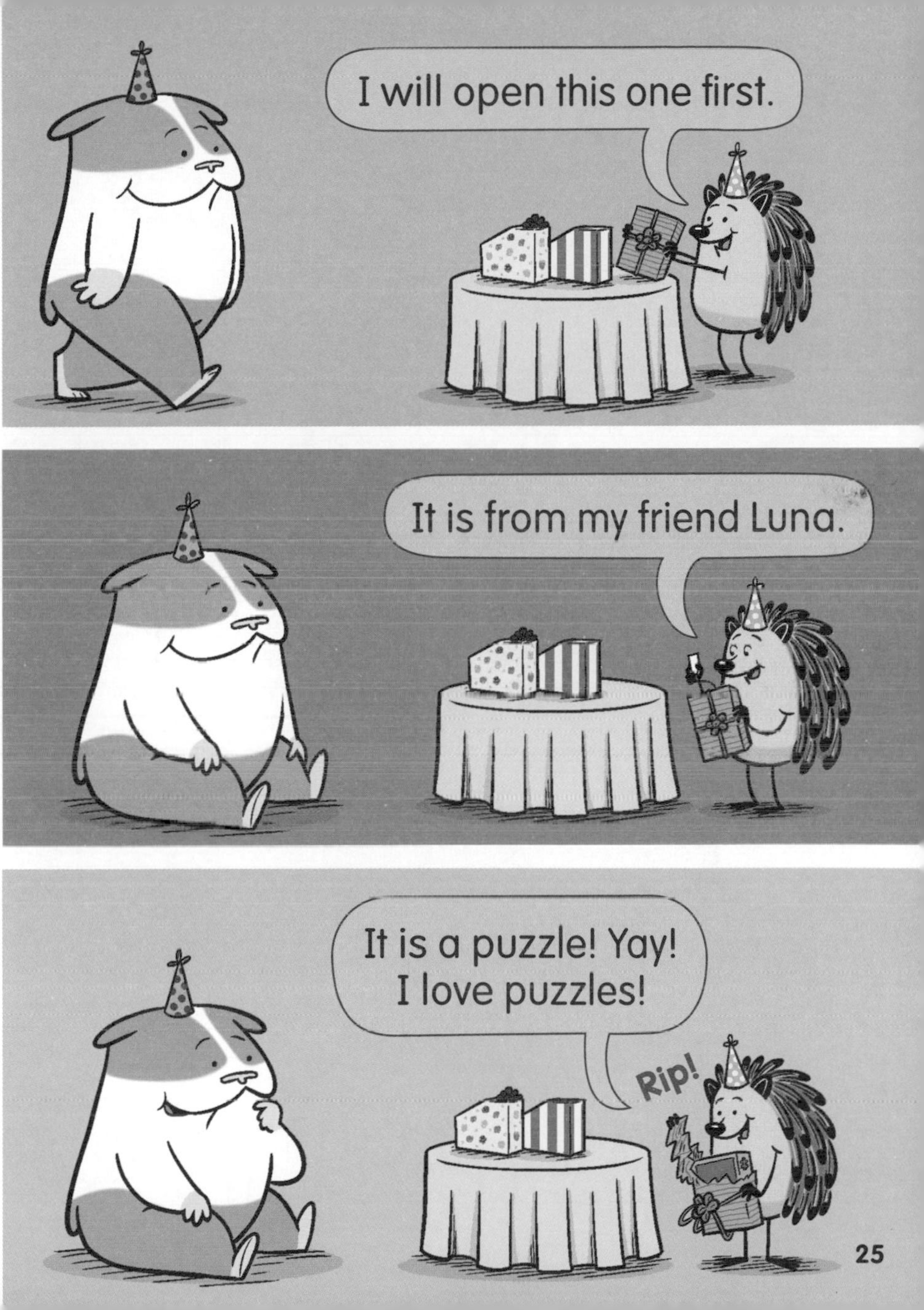
I will open this one first.
It is from my friend Luna.
It is a puzzle! Yay! I love puzzles!
Rip!

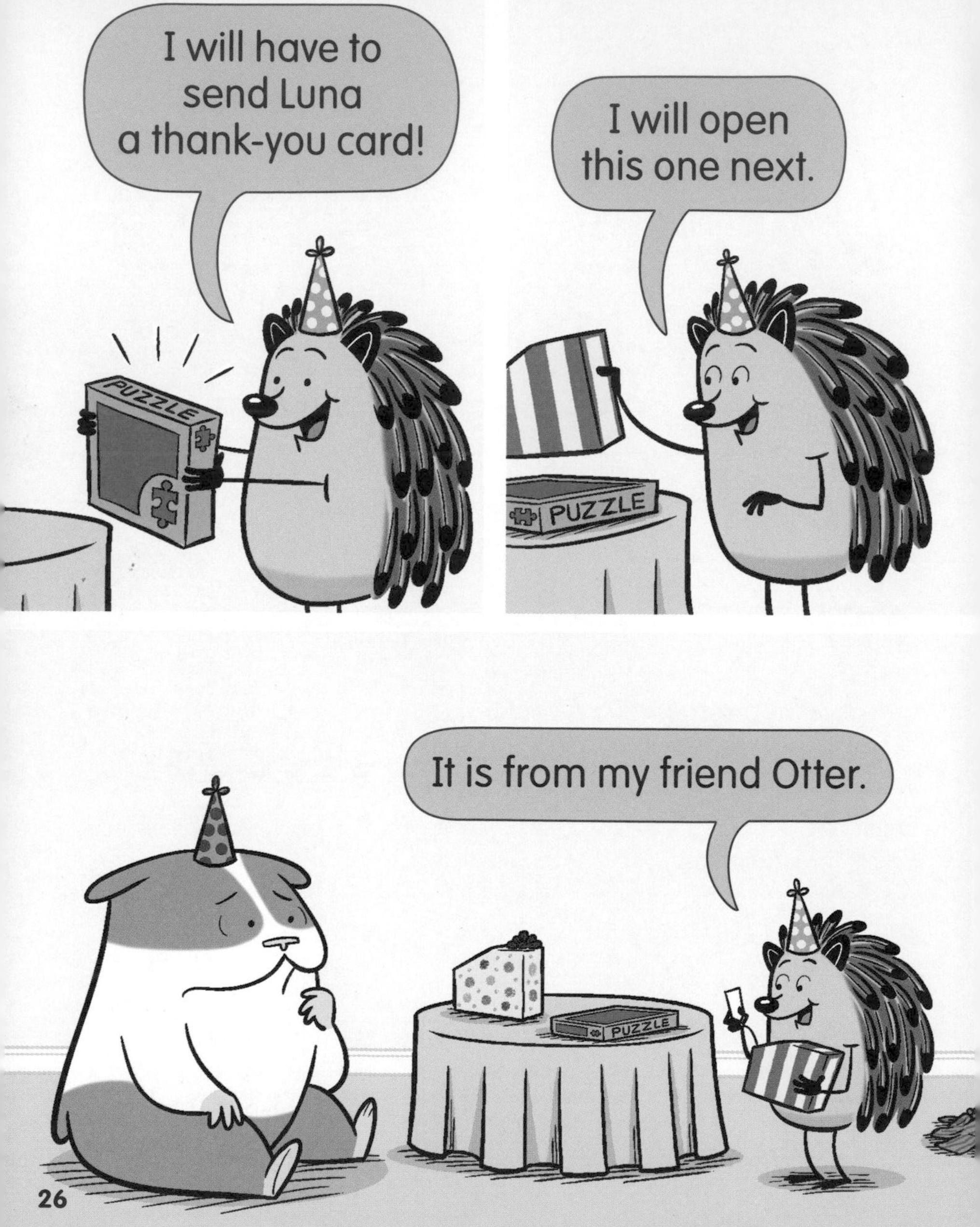
I will have to send Luna a thank-you card!
PUZZLE
I will open this one next.
PUZZLE
It is from my friend Otter.
PUZZLE

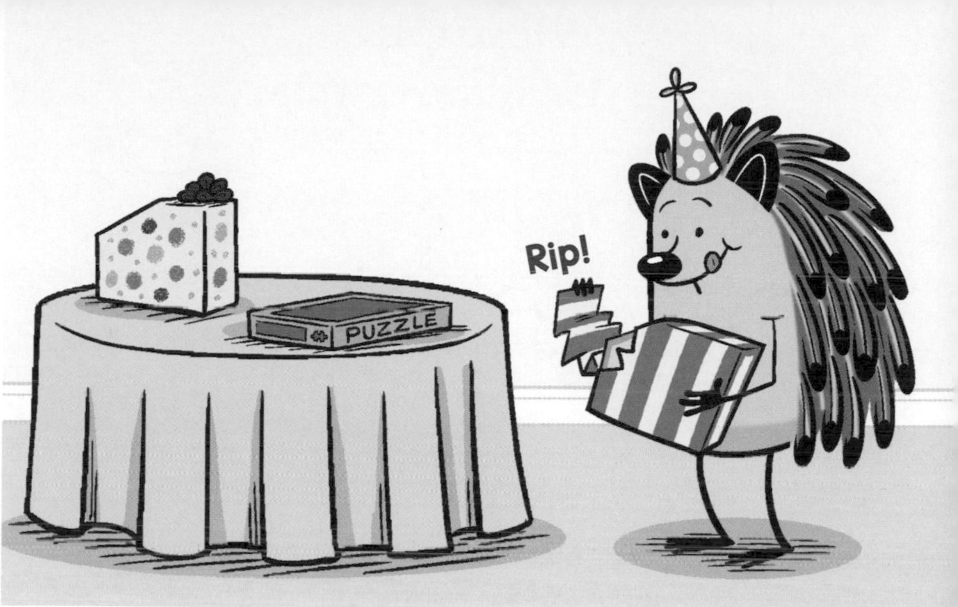
PUZZLE
Rip!

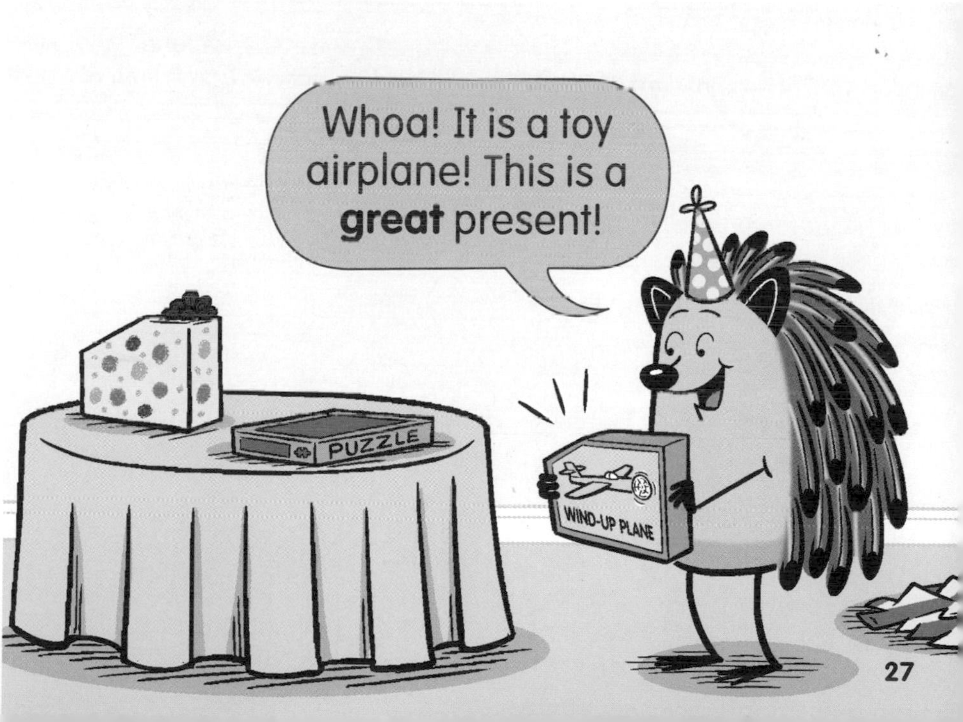
Whoa! It is a toy airplane! This is a **great** present!
PUZZLE
WIND-UP PLANE

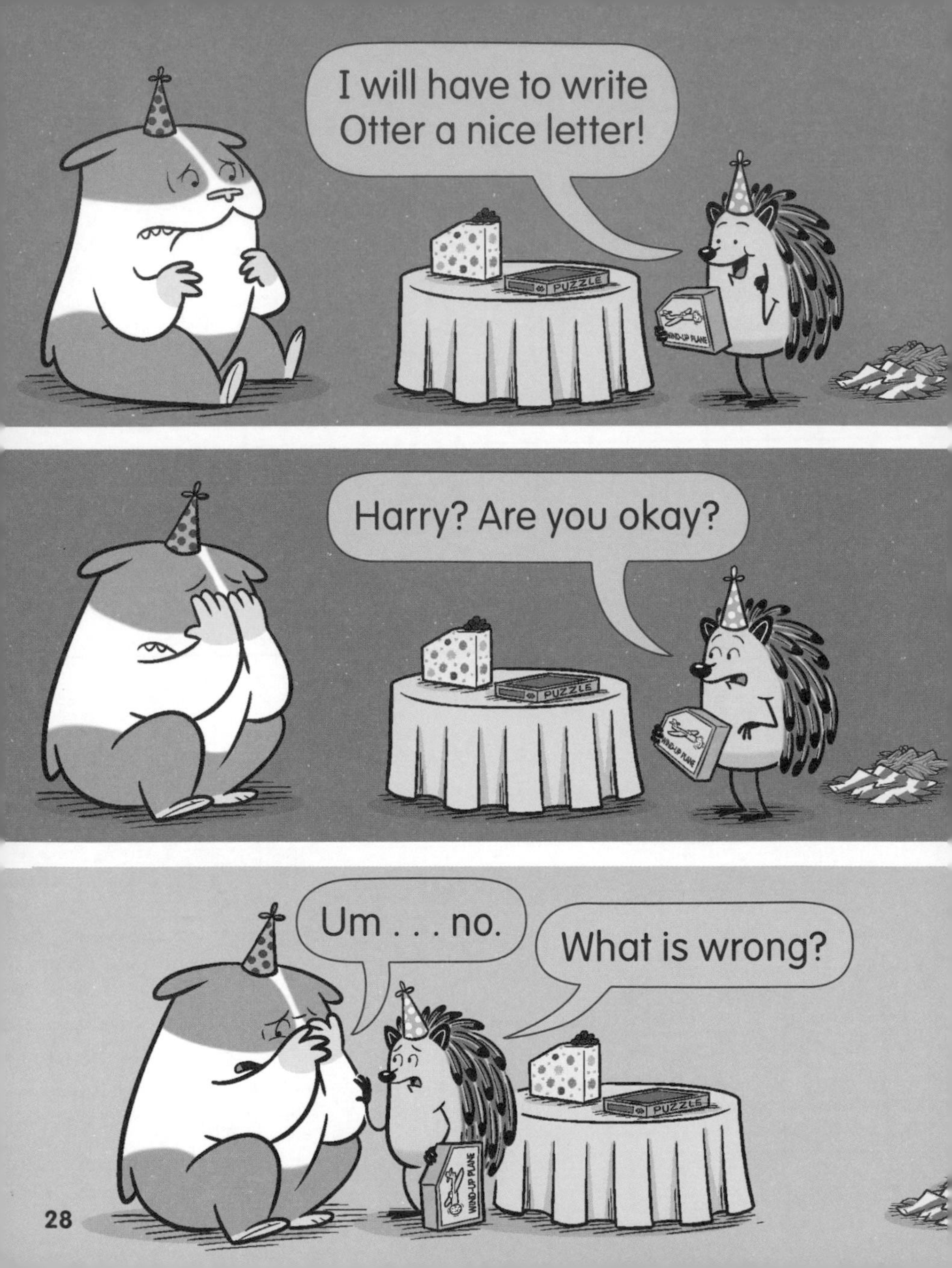
I will have to write Otter a nice letter!
PUZZLE
WIND-UP PLANE
Harry? Are you okay?
PUZZLE
WIND-UP PLANE
Um . . . no.
What is wrong?
PUZZLE
WIND-UP PLANE

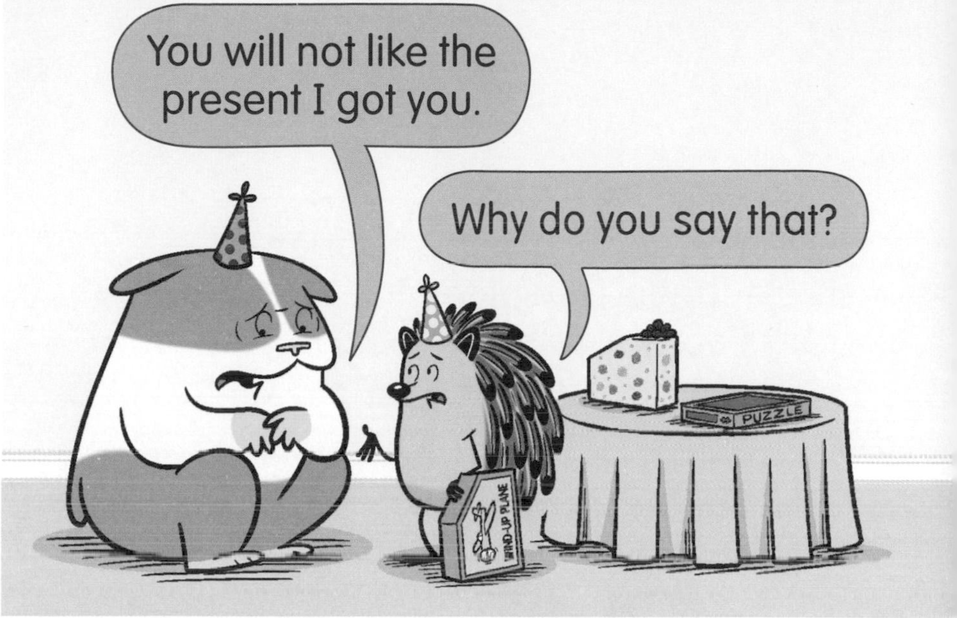
You will not like the present I got you.
Why do you say that?
WIND-UP PLANE
PUZZLE

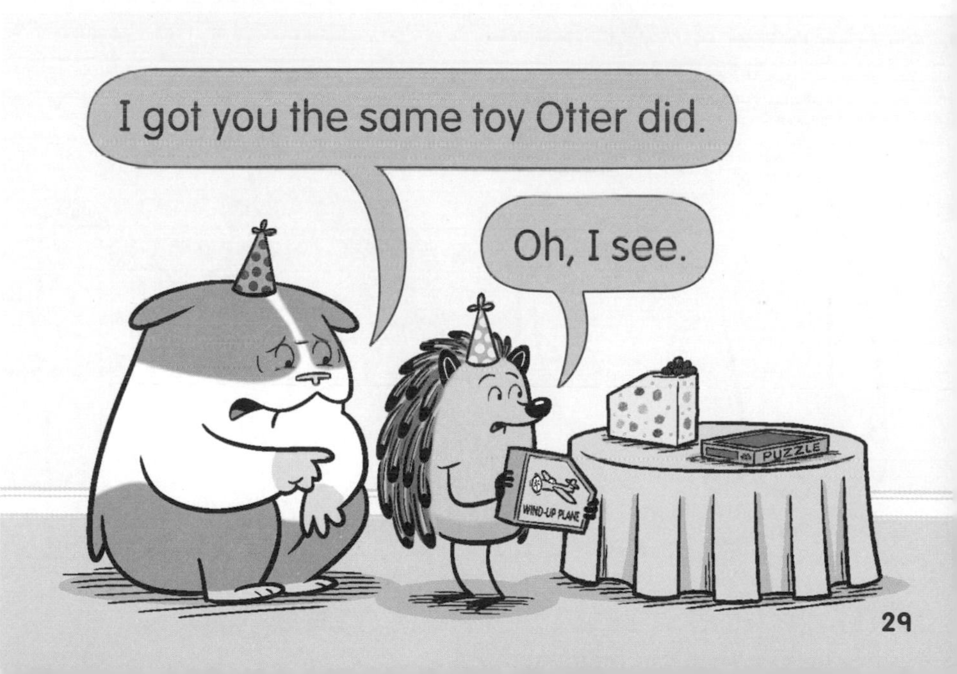
I got you the same toy Otter did.
Oh, I see.
WIND-UP PLANE
PUZZLE

You are such a special friend, Hedgehog. I wanted the present I got you to be the best one.
But, Harry, your present is the best one!
WIND-UP PLANE

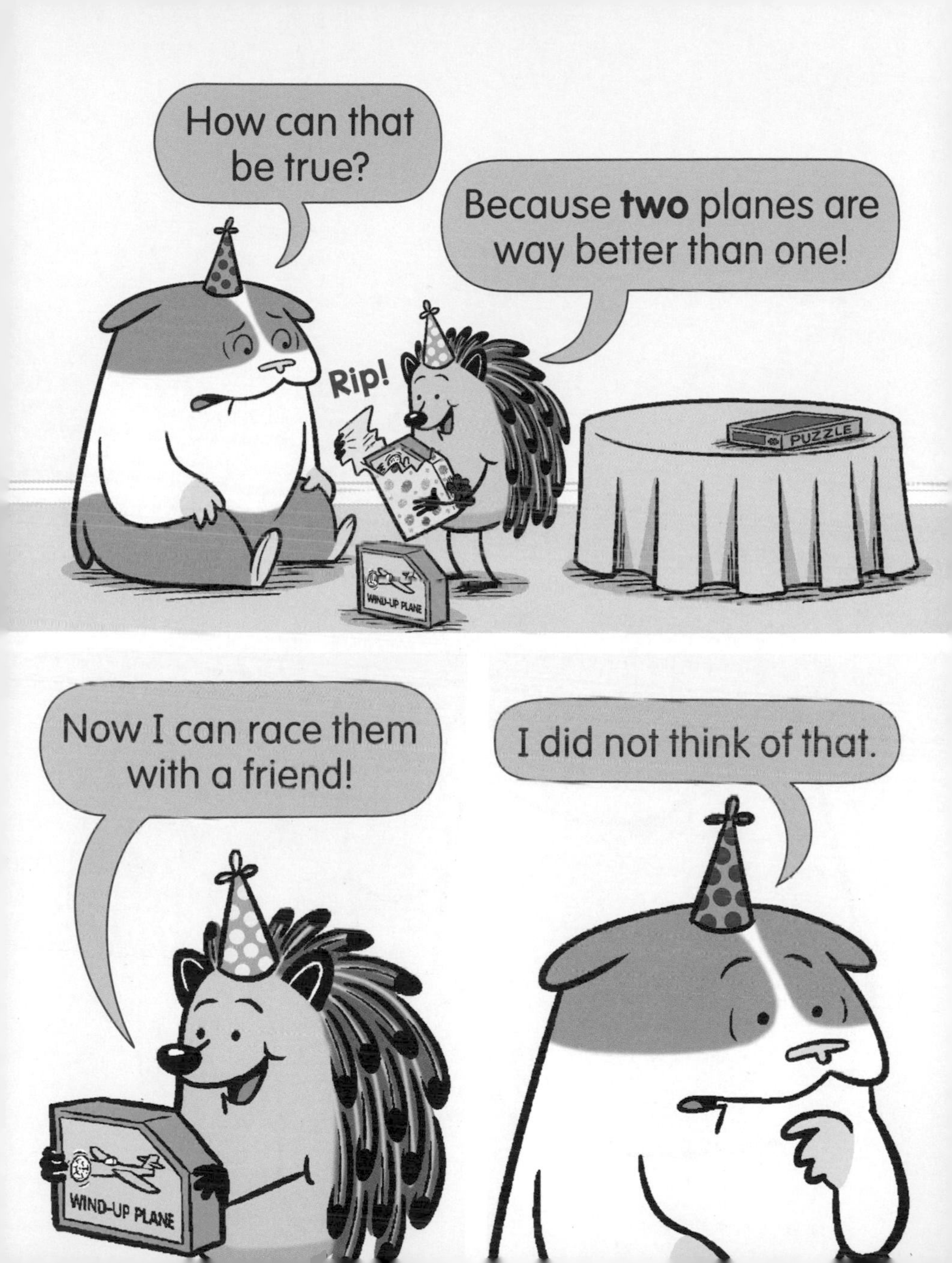
How can that be true?
Because **two** planes are way better than one!
Rip!
PUZZLE
WIND-UP PLANE
Now I can race them with a friend!
I did not think of that.
WIND-UP PLANE

You are a good friend, Hedgehog.
You are my **best** friend, Harry.
WIND-UP PLANE
WIND-UP PLANE

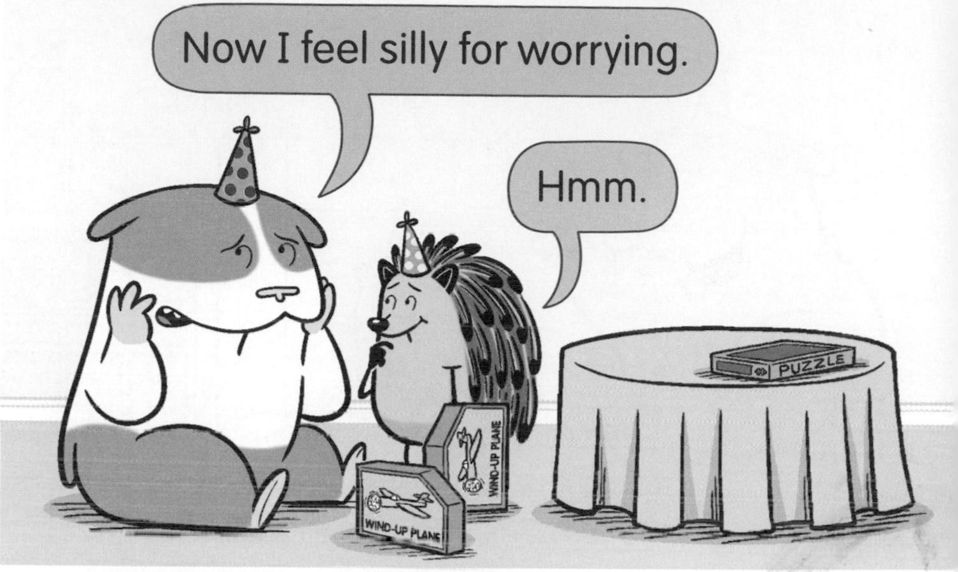
Now I feel silly for worrying.
Hmm.
PUZZLE
WIND-UP PLANE
WIND-UP PLANE

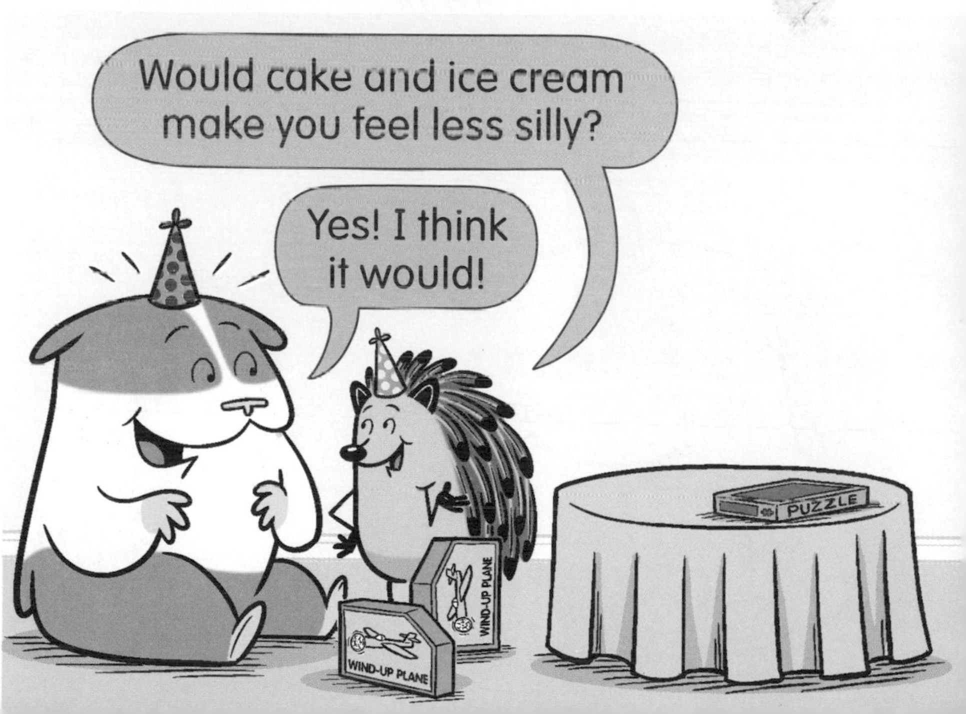
Would cake and ice cream make you feel less silly?
Yes! I think it would!
PUZZLE
WIND-UP PLANE
WIND-UP PLANE

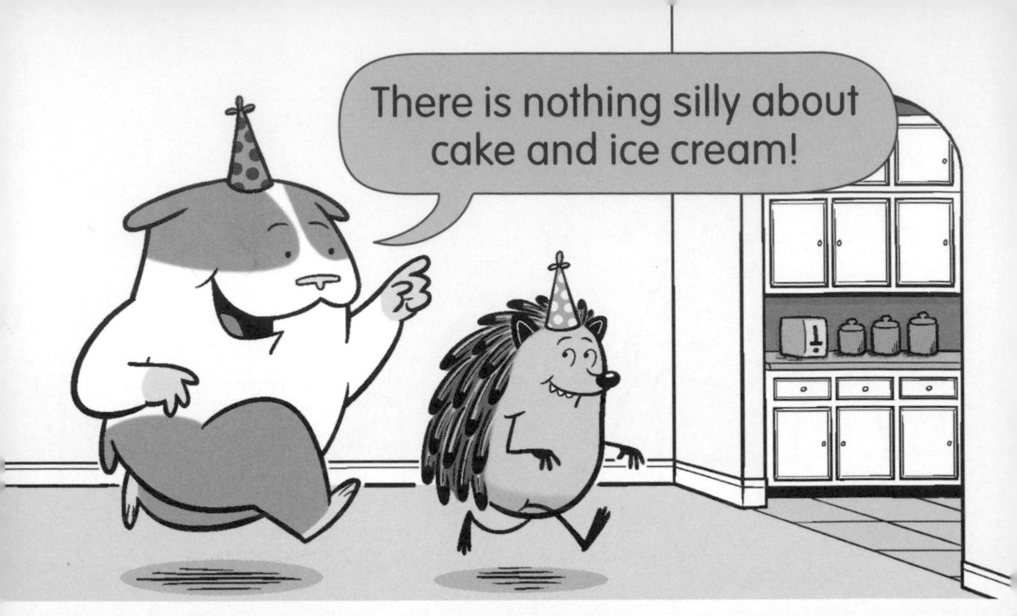
There is nothing silly about cake and ice cream!

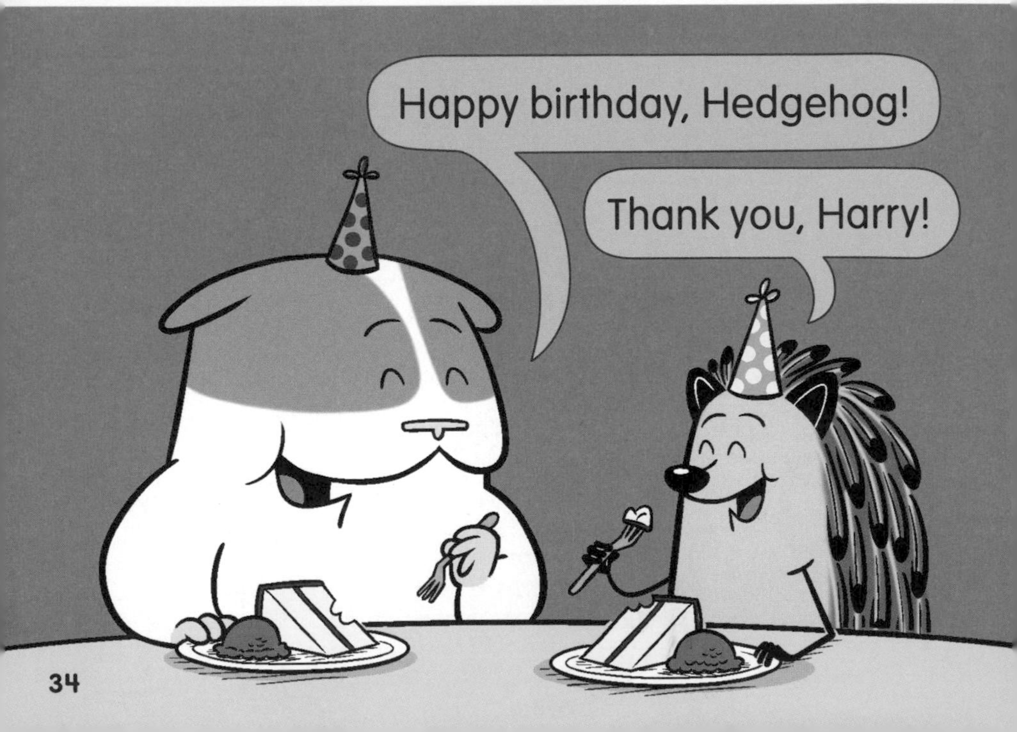
Happy birthday, Hedgehog!
Thank you, Harry!

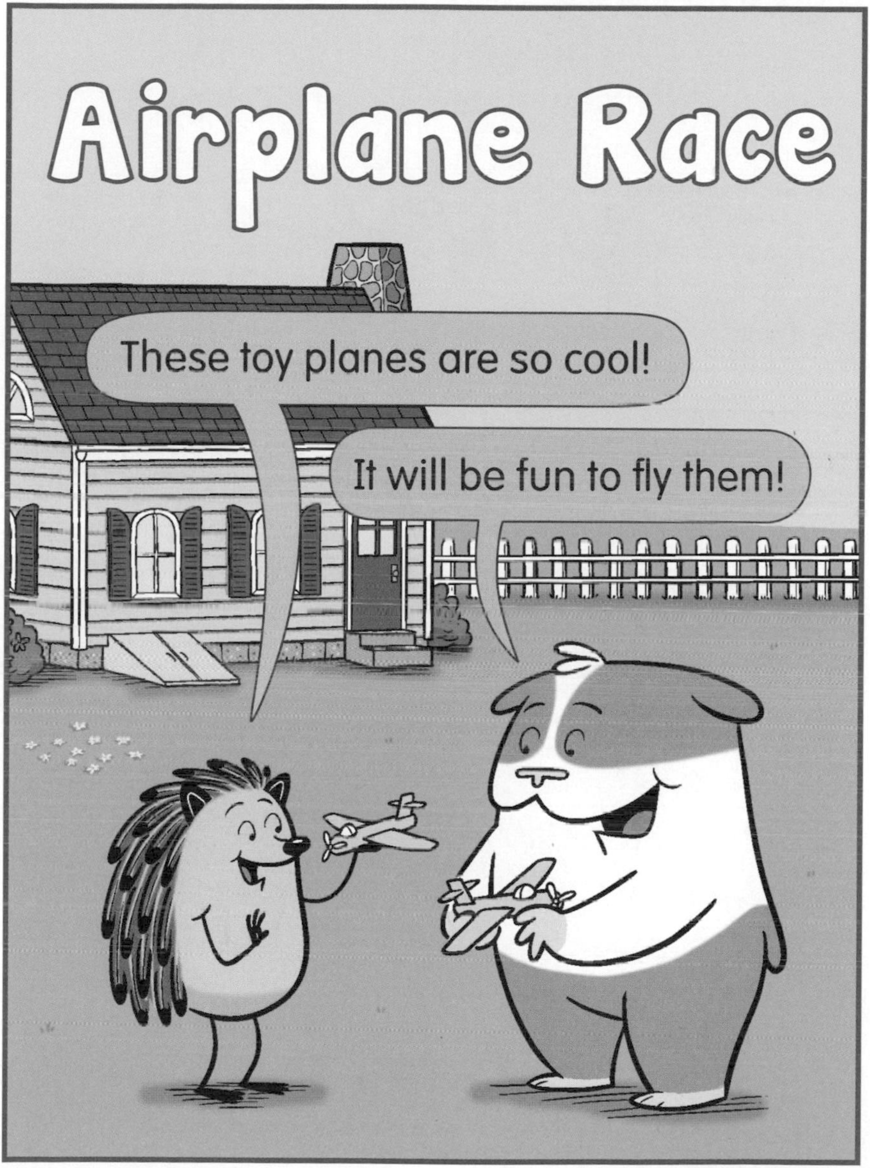
Airplane Race
These toy planes are so cool!
It will be fun to fly them!

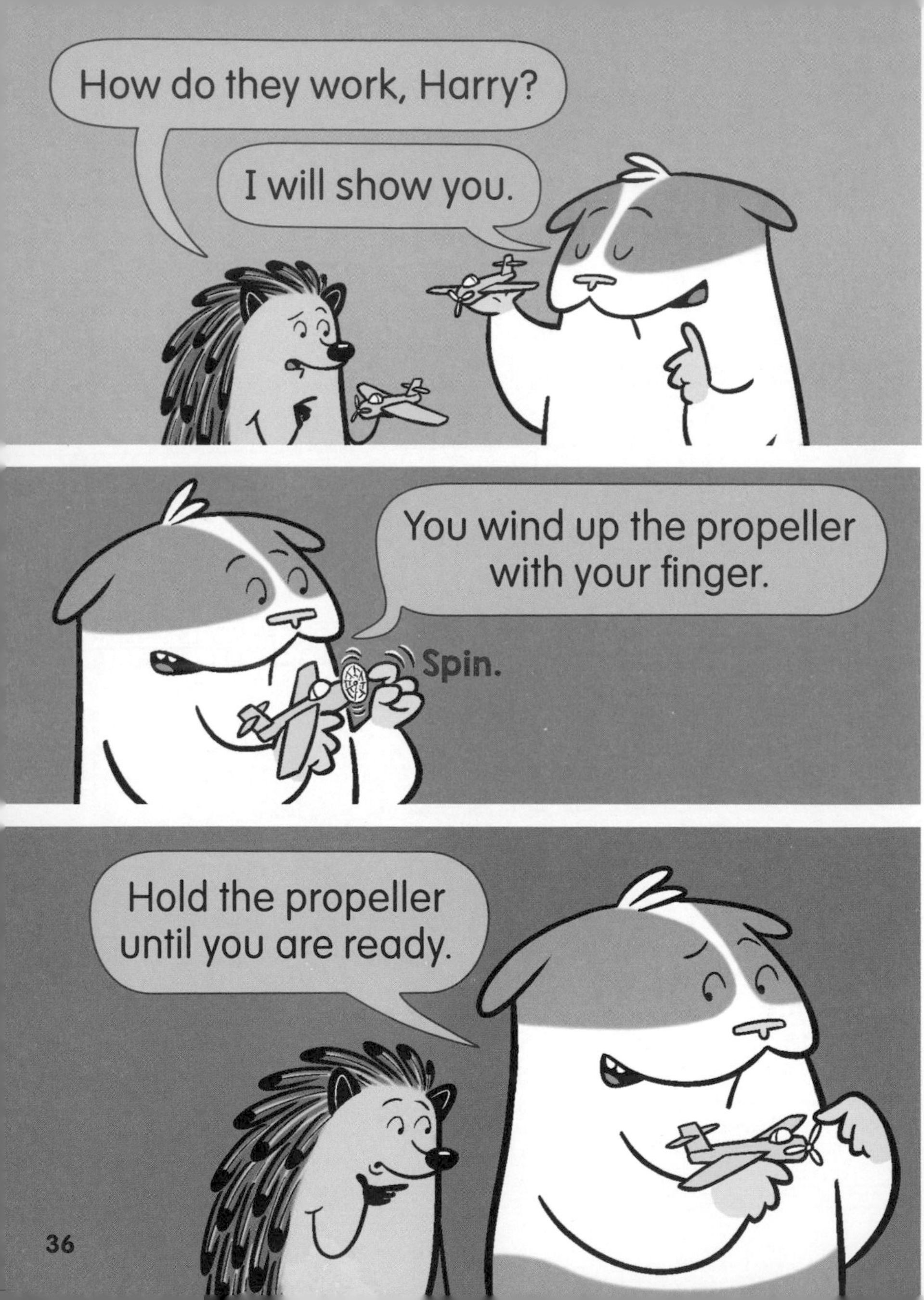
How do they work, Harry?
I will show you.
You wind up the propeller with your finger.
Spin.
Hold the propeller until you are ready.

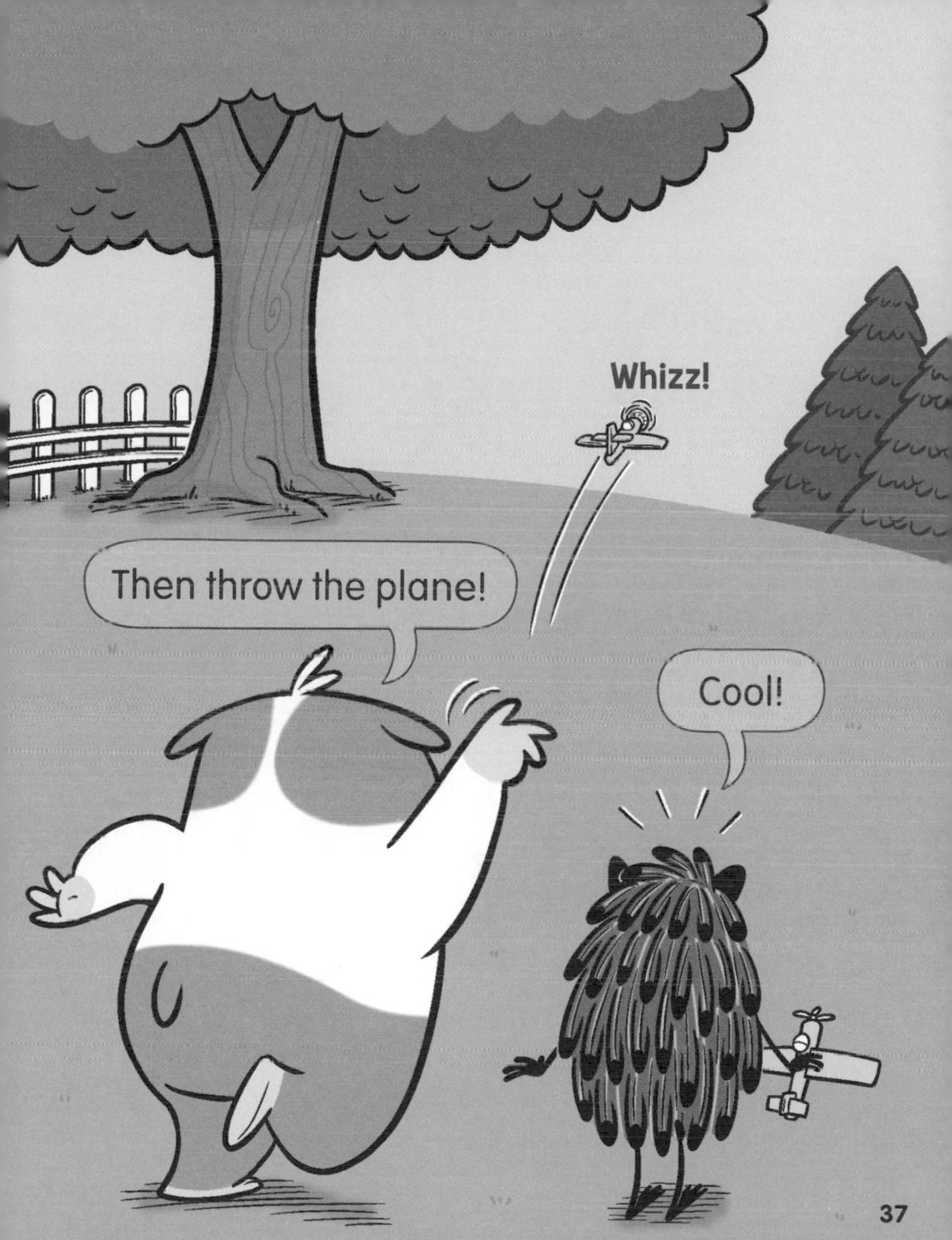
Whizz!
Then throw the plane!
Cool!

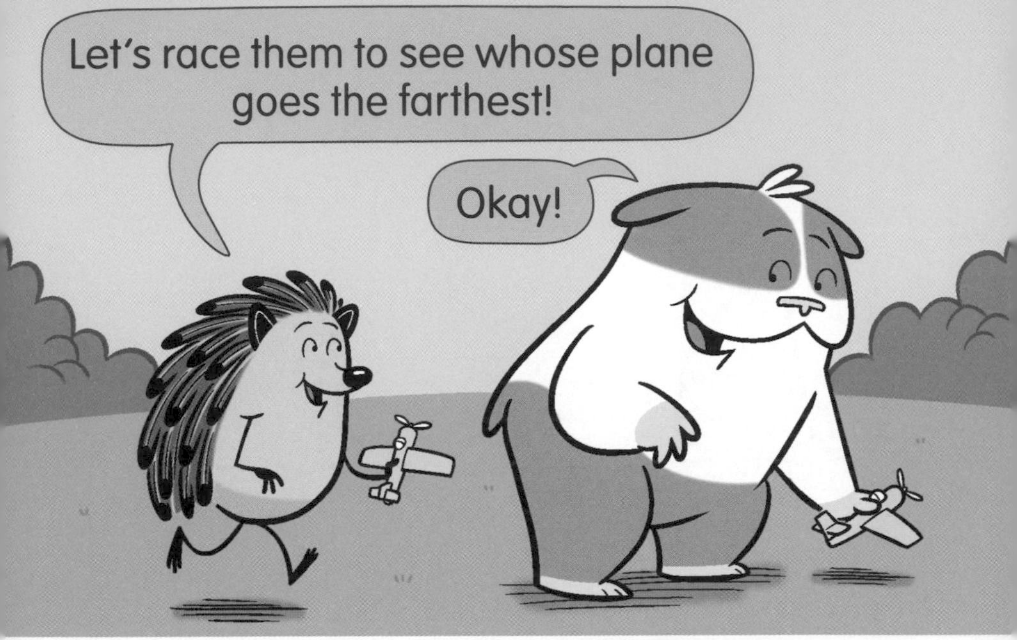
Let's race them to see whose plane goes the farthest!
Okay!

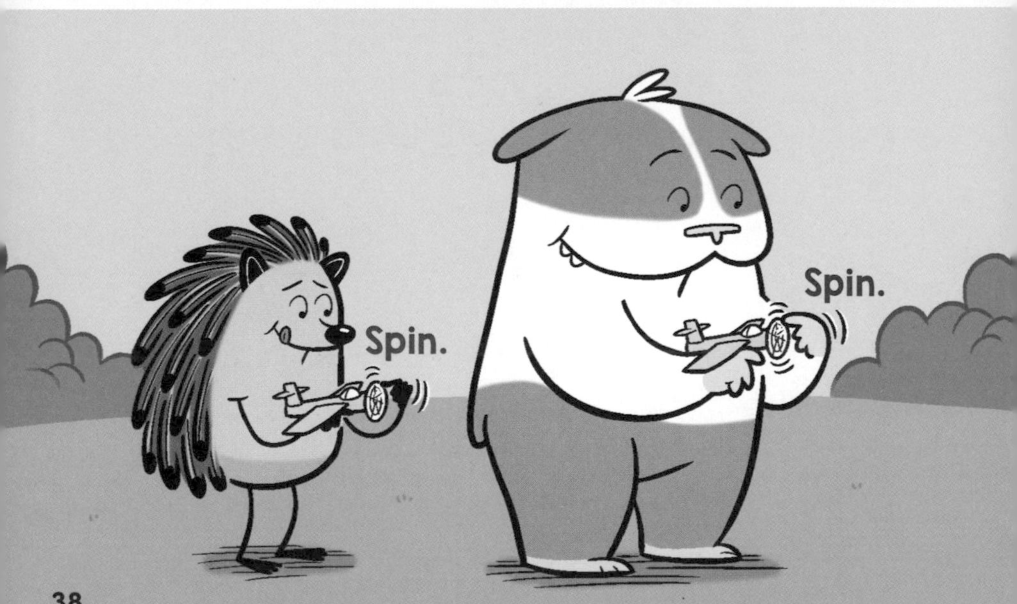
Spin.
Spin.

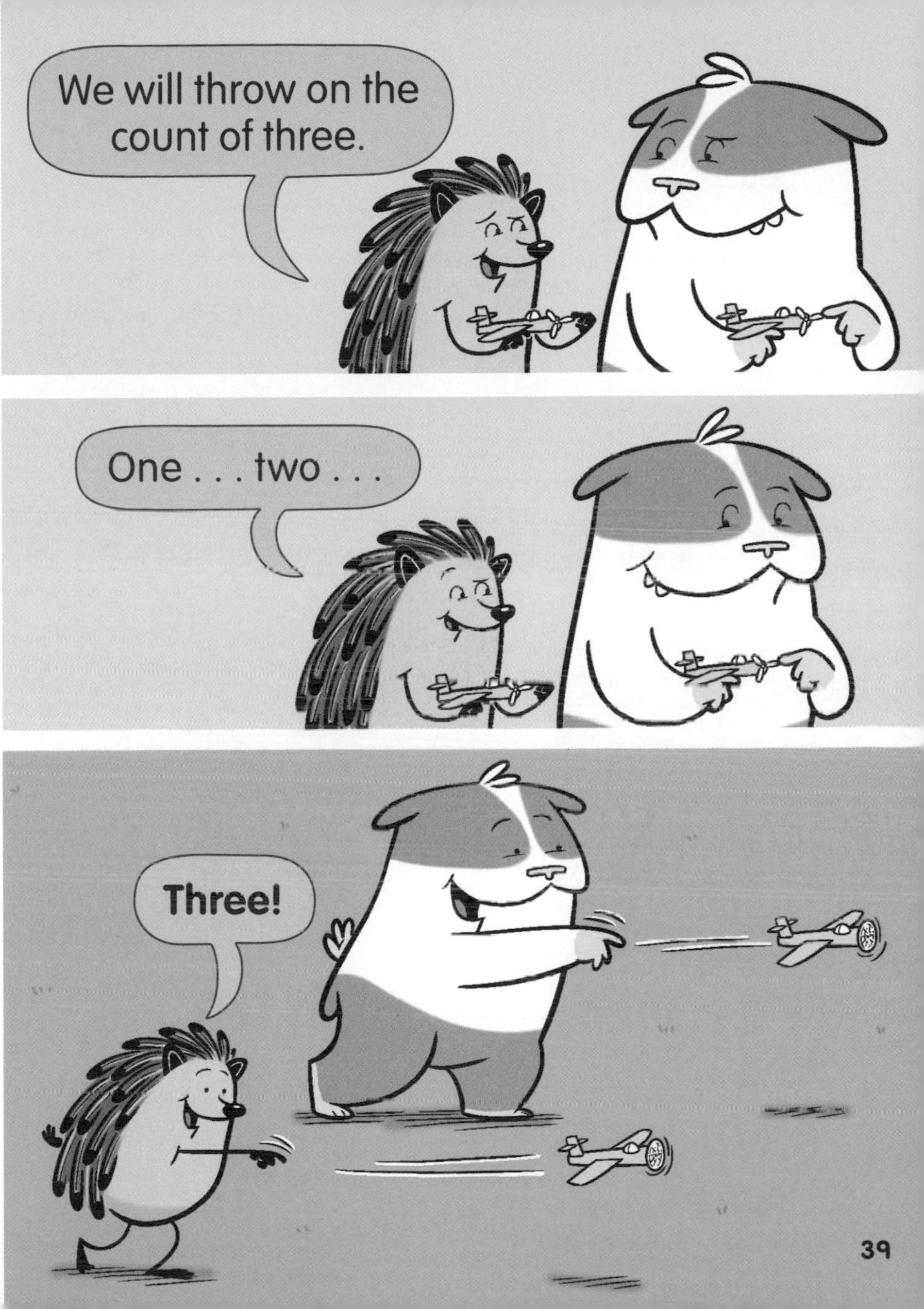
We will throw on the count of three.
One . . . two . . .
Three!

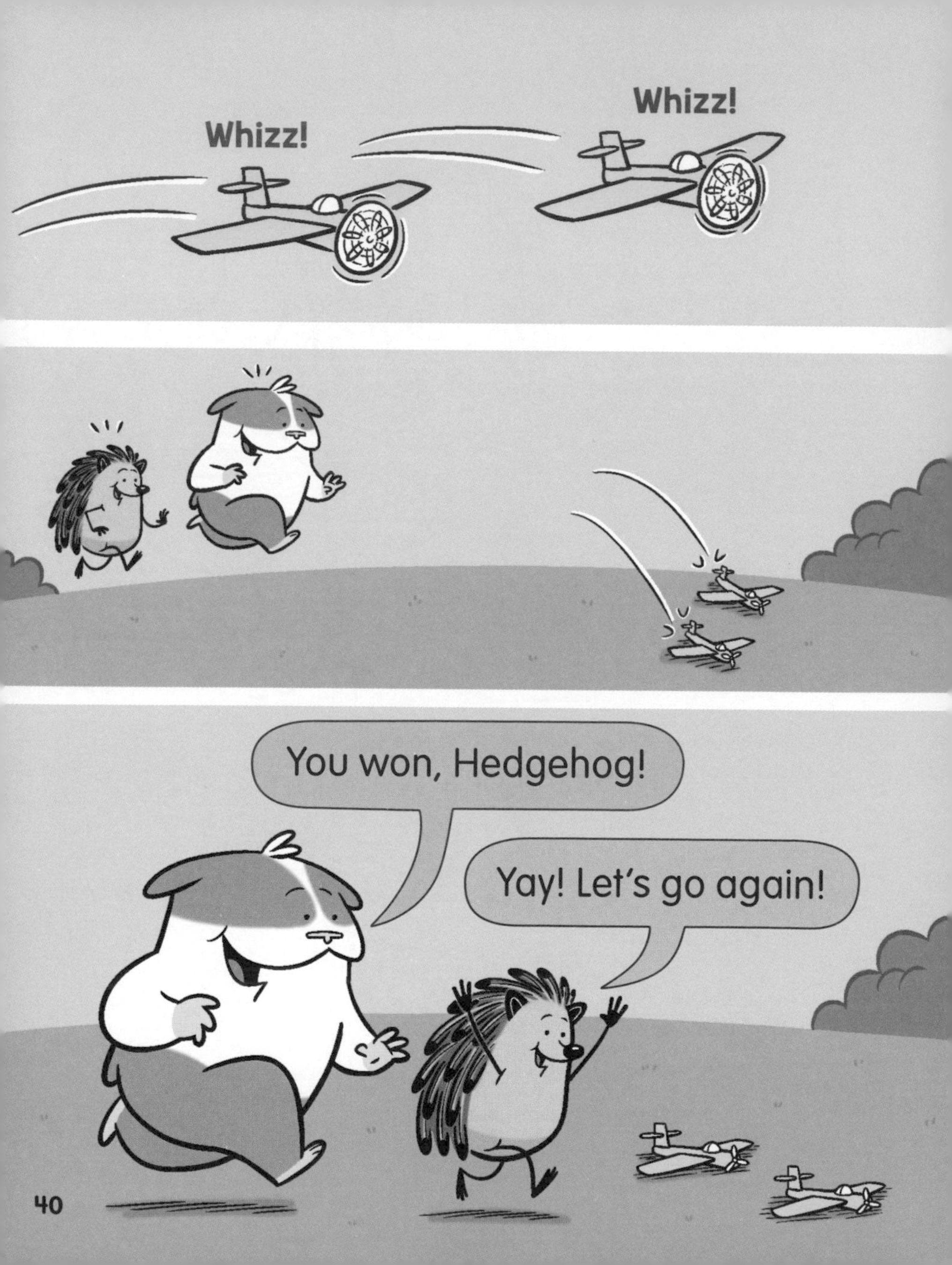
Whizz!
Whizz!
You won, Hedgehog!
Yay! Let's go again!

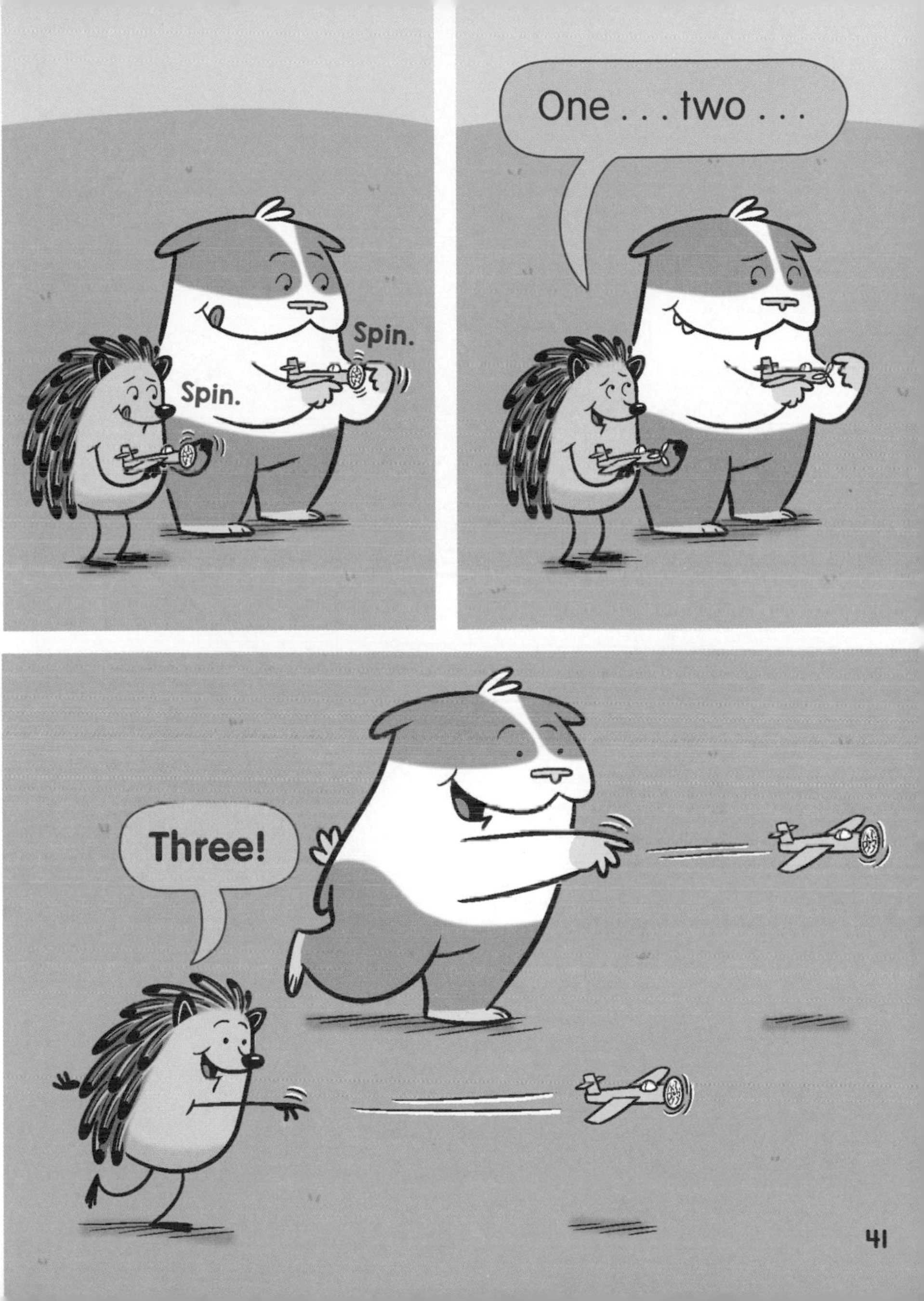
Spin.
Spin.
One . . . two . . .
Three!

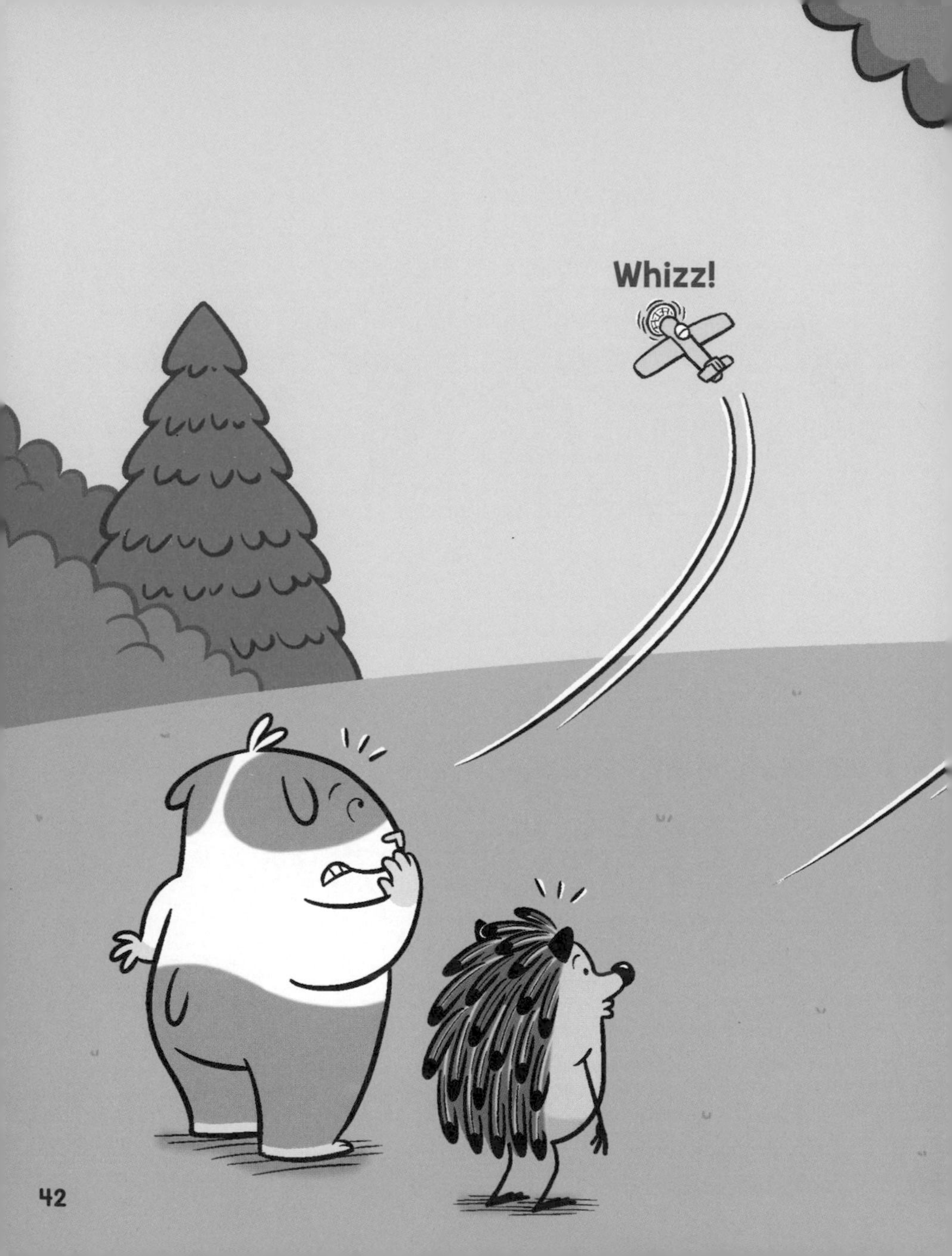
Whizz!

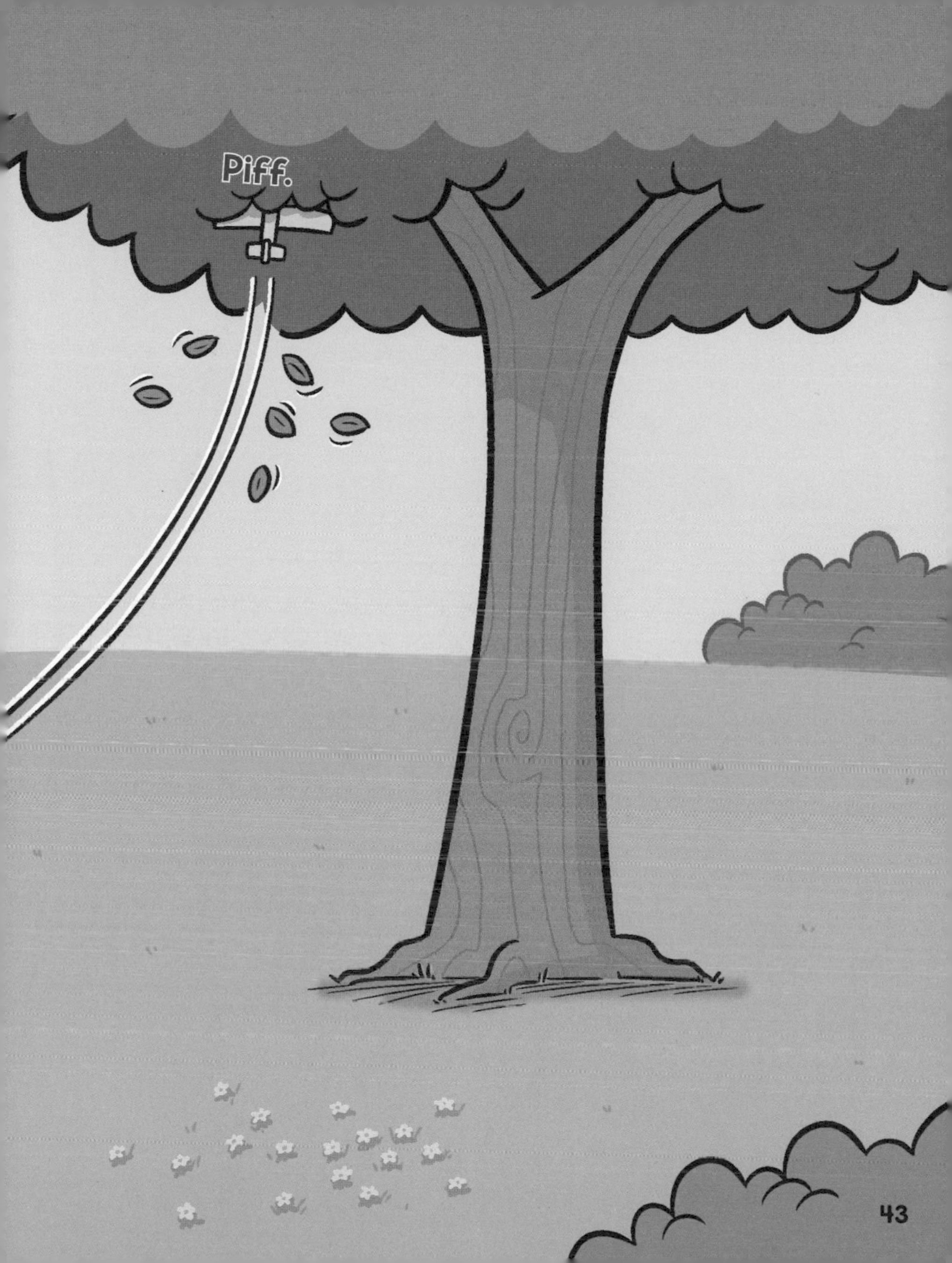
Piff.

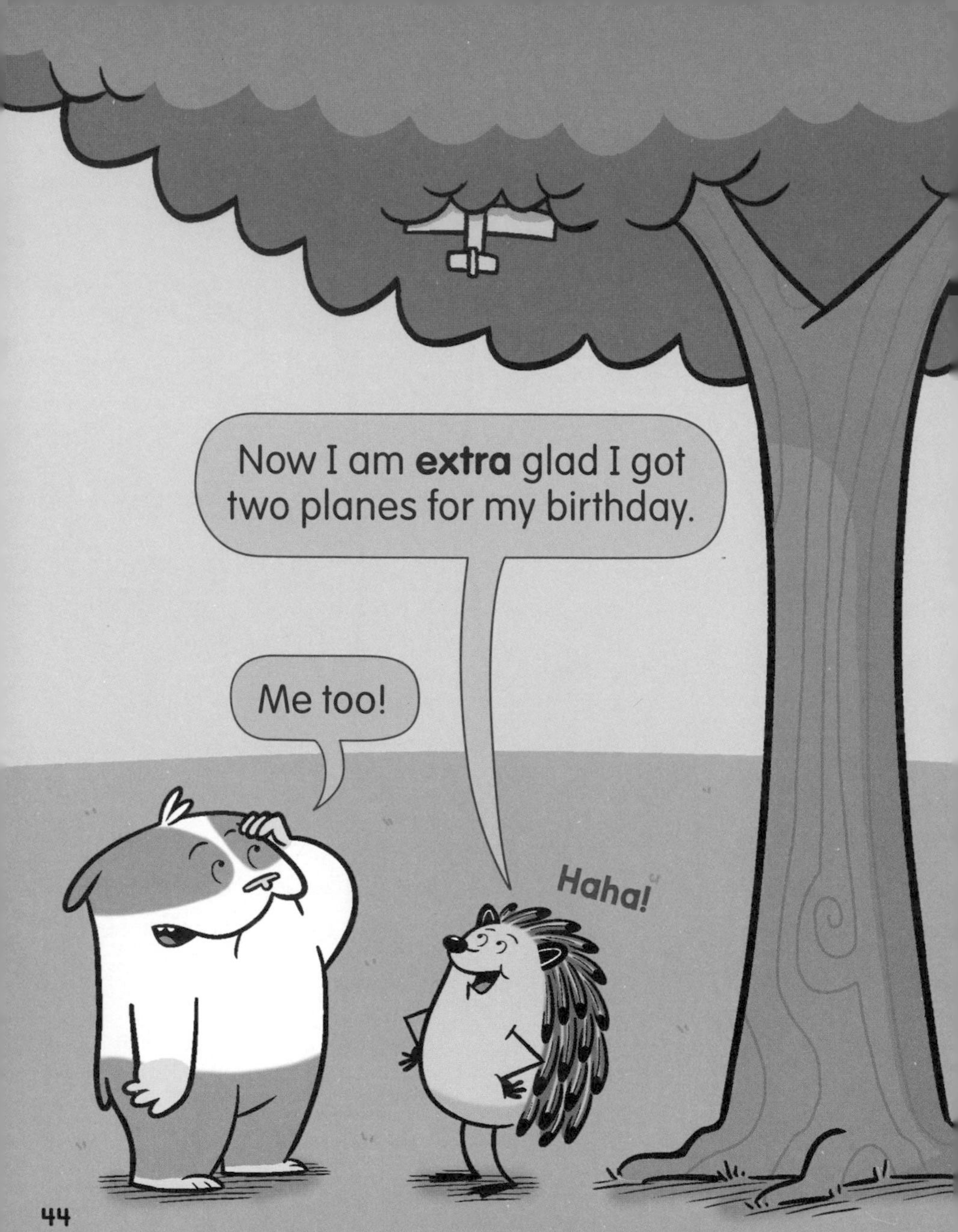
Now I am **extra** glad I got two planes for my birthday.
Me too!
Haha!

About the Author

Norm Feuti lives in Massachusetts with his family, a dog, two cats, and a guinea pig. He is the creator of the newspaper comic strips **Retail** and **Gil**. He is also the author and illustrator of the graphic novel series **Beak and Ally**. **Hello, Hedgehog!** is Norm's first early reader series.

YOU CAN DRAW HEDGEHOG!

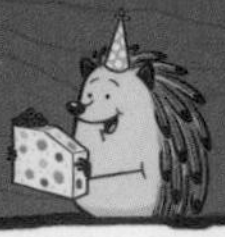

1. Draw a jelly bean shape.

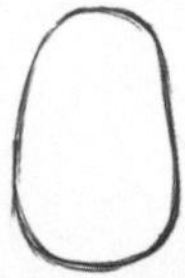

2. Add the eyes, ears, nose, and mouth.

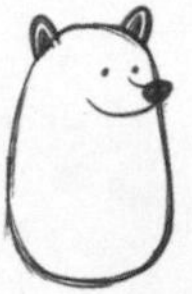

3. Draw a triangle hat, and a box shape.

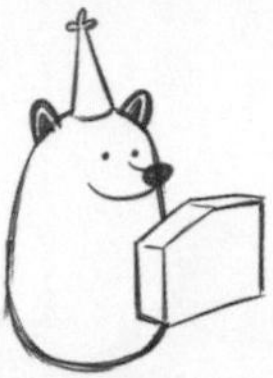

4. Give Hedgehog arms, legs and lots of quills. Put black spots on the ends of the quills.

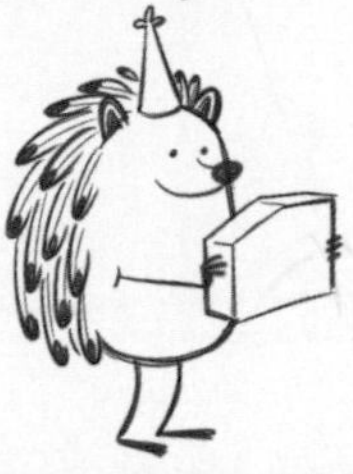

5. Draw the eyebrows, a big smile, and put a bow on the present.

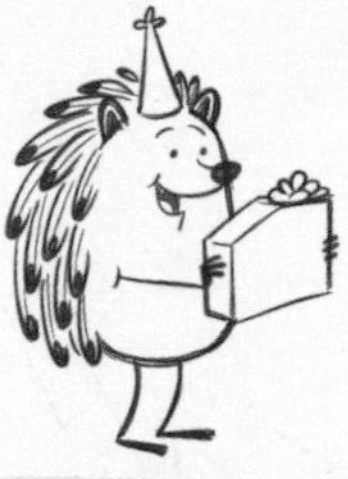

6. Color in your drawing!

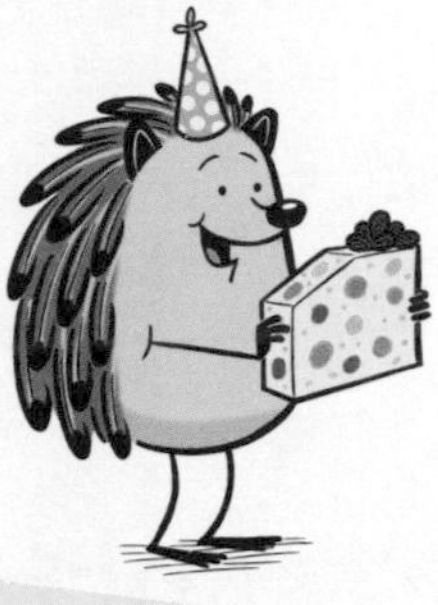

WHAT'S YOUR STORY?

It is Hedgehog's birthday! Harry gives him a present.
Imagine **you** go to Hedgehog's birthday party.
What present would you bring? Would you wrap it?
What party games would you play?
Write and draw your story!

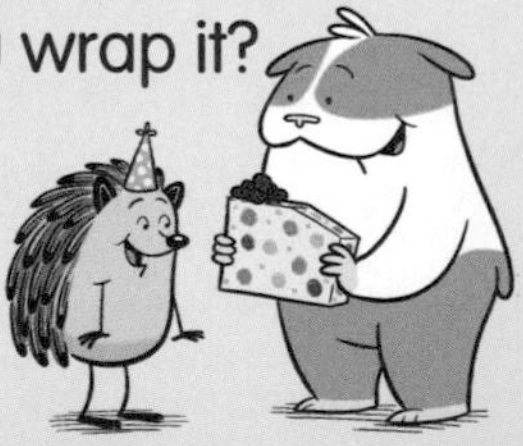

scholastic.com/acorn